THE SAGE'S CONSORT

KRYSTAL N CRAIKER

Printed in the United States of America

First Printing, 2019

ISBN 978-1-7340767-3-8

Published by Krystal N. Craiker

krystalncraiker.com

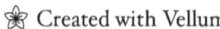 Created with Vellum

To Michael

ACKNOWLEDGMENTS

My beta readers, Lorraine Hall, Elizabeth Kaupisch, and Pinar Tarhan, were honest, timely, and encouraging. Thank you.

My mother, Kathy Craiker, is always my number one fan and believes in me. I appreciated her constant texts as she got to new parts of the book.

And finally, my rock, my support, the love of my life, thank you Michael Dunn. Thank you for supporting me through this endeavor, emotionally and financially. Thanks for fetching me caffeine and reassuring me when I cried. Thank you for loving me even though I spend roughly 75% of my time in my made-up worlds. I love you.

MAP OF ELANDRIA

PROLOGUE

A crisp breeze blew across the autumn night, and with it a nefarious darkness crept into the otherwise peaceful country. Throughout Elandria, most of the population slept serenely, unaware of the evil that had taken root. Even the king snored in content, as he did most nights. Ruling Elandria was an easy job; no major conflicts had occurred in hundreds of years, and the king left most of the legislating to his parliament.

But this night, Scholars across the land tossed and turned in their beds. Some slept plagued by random nightmares they would not remember. Others woke after midnight and never fell back to sleep. Still others never slept; their most powerful sleeping draughts could not combat tonight's insomnia. Upon waking, they would find that every Scholar they knew slept restlessly the night before. They would find no reason and would write it off as simply a shift in the climate.

⁂

A YOUNG STUDENT dreamed in his dormitory at the Academy for Scholars in the capital city of Teleah. A crushing black force approached him. At first, he stood trying to examine the encroaching nothingness, his Scholar's curiosity present even in his unconscious state. But it swept toward him, faster, and he felt a fear he had never known before. He ran. The darkness followed. He ran faster. The darkness quickened. He ran until he could not breathe and his side ached from the strain. No longer able to resist, he closed his eyes as the darkness enveloped him. As the evil swallowed him whole, he felt a pain in his heart, as if it were ripped from his chest. He cried out, and then, there was nothing.

Quinn bolted upright in his bed, sweat dripping from his brow. His heart pounded like a thousand off-beat drums in his chest. He clawed at his heart and forced himself to calm as his eyes adjusted to the dark room. He studied his dormitory, trying to find his way back to reality. A glint of moonlight shone through the window. His bedclothes were tangled and soaked through with his sweat. His books were stacked neatly on his desk where he had left them. You're in your dorm, he told himself. It was only a dream.

But it felt like so much more than a dream. It felt more like a warning or perhaps a prophecy, a message. There's no such thing, he reasoned with his racing mind. It was a nightmare and nothing more. Quinn untangled himself from his sheets and placed his feet on the cold stone floor. He glanced at Rafe, his roommate. Rafe had somehow turned himself upside down in his sleep; his feet rested on his pillow and his head hung off the end of the bed. He grunted and twitched. It was odd, Quinn noticed, because normally Rafe slept like the dead.

Quinn crossed the dark room to the washbasin. He splashed cold water on his face, trying to shake off the last of his dream state. He had class early in the morning and knew he should try to get some more sleep. He squinted at the clock on his nightstand: just after two o'clock in the morning. He sighed. He felt an irrational anxiety at falling back to sleep; the nightmare threatened to follow him. He resigned himself to insomnia and picked up the Sage's latest publication on the holiday rituals of the Deyoni people. He read in his bed until the black night became a pale grey, finally falling asleep for the last hour or two before dawn.

JUST OUTSIDE TELEAH, halfway up a sloping green mountain, the Sage of Elandria stood on her balcony, searching the night for something, anything. She strained her eyes and chewed her lip, looking for an approaching dark nothingness. She had woken from something more than a dream, something intangible that filled her with fear and despair. In her sleep, something evil had swallowed her, making her cry out in pain. She had awoken, breathless and shaking, shortly after two o'clock in the morning.

Her head ached with knowledge that something was deeply wrong in Elandria. Most Scholars put little stock in dreams, but she knew that this was more. For the last three hundred years, Elandria had flourished in peace, but she knew in her heart something had changed.

After an hour, she convinced herself to return inside to her warm bed. Even if a mysterious darkness was approaching, standing on her balcony would do no good. She wondered if she should send word to the Academy and to the king. She decided to wait. She may wield the strongest earth magic in the land, but she doubted if anyone cared about her nightmares.

As she drifted back to sleep, she remembered the strangest part of her dream. She had called out to someone as she crumbled under the force of the darkness, but in her conscious state, she could not recall the name. It rested at the back of her thoughts, just out of reach.

MILES AWAY, something evil encroached on a small fishing village on the Great Silver Lake. Nothing eventful ever happened here. The people went about their lives, selling their fish to the cities and towns nearby. Strangers were welcomed openly, including the two Scholars visiting to identify the Gift of the Earth in the local children.

The back door of the local inn blew open in the autumn wind. A stranger, known to no one in town, had entered quietly after the last of the patrons retired for the night. He did not latch the door behind him. He climbed the stairs, careful not to make a noise, and picked the lock to the second room on the right.

The two Scholars lay in their single beds in restless slumber. The stranger drew his knife and quickly slit their throats. He lingered a moment, watching the blood pool around them, drenching their Scholar's pendants in red. Pleased with himself, he murmured a quiet word of thanks into the night and crept quietly back down the stairs and into the darkness.

CHAPTER 1

A sharp pain in his side jolted Quinn awake. Rafe had elbowed him in the ribcage. Quinn blinked, trying to regain his senses. He sat in Professor Quickthorn's lecture hall, an ancient stone chamber lit only by lanterns, which made staying awake even more difficult today. He had never fallen asleep in class before.

To his left, Rafe seemed to be trying too hard to pay attention. Quinn noticed his roommate had failed to lace his shirt this morning and his long, dark locks were uncombed. On Rafe's other side, Sarah stared off into the distance, twirling her golden hair with a glazed look in her eyes. To Quinn's right, Jack had fallen asleep with his head on the desk, mouth slightly open, a trail of saliva leaking onto the wooden surface.

Every student Scholar appeared dazed and tired. Jack was not the only person asleep. Quinn would have assumed the end of the school year and the approaching exams were causing everyone a new level of exhaustion. But both Rafe and Jack had mentioned how restless their nights had been, although they remembered no nightmares like Quinn. Even Quickthorn seemed tired. The elderly Scholar could barely complete a sentence without yawning. Quinn could see dark bags under her eyes even from several rows back, and loose strands of grey fell out of her normally tight hair bun. The slight woman leaned against the oak podium as if to support herself.

"Oh, forget it," Quickthorn said. "The last hundred years of history are boring, anyway. Finish reading the chapter before the next class. It will appear on your exams. Class dismissed." She yawned again. Across the stone chamber, awake students nudged their sleeping friends. Quinn elbowed Jack as hard as he could. Jack grunted in surprise.

"You're disgusting, Jack." Quinn pointed at the puddle of drool his friend had left on the desk. Rafe snickered. "Clean that up. Quickthorn let us out early." The young men gathered their books. Quinn had a full hour before his next class. He wondered if he could get a quick nap in before. Then he remembered his dream from the night before and shuddered. Perhaps he would find some strong coffee instead.

"Mr. Atwell," Quickthorn said. Quinn looked up at his professor. "Would you escort me to my office? I'd like to talk to you." Or maybe the coffee would have to wait. He nodded. Rafe gave him an inquiring look; Quinn just shrugged.

He followed the elderly Scholar out of the lecture hall and down the stone steps into the courtyard. He blinked; the sun seemed abnormally bright today. Normally, the old stone walls echoed with chatter and laughing of student Scholars. Today it seemed unusually quiet. He saw multiple students asleep on benches or under the shade of the red and yellow-leaved trees; indeed, of the few people in the courtyard, most were in varying states of sleep. Quinn wondered if he had been the only one to have that dream last night. People don't have the same dreams, he told himself. Even Scholars.

Quickthorn walked fast for someone her age. She was small and the most wrinkled woman he had ever seen. Her features were sharp, but her manners were soft. She was Quinn's favorite professor and his academic mentor. Her history and culture classes had always been his favorite, and Professor Quickthorn had so many stories and experiences that he found her courses captivating.

Across the courtyard, Quinn followed his professor through the large wooden doors that led to a corridor of offices. She opened her office door and gestured at Quinn to take a seat. He was no stranger to this room; as her mentee, he met with her several times a year to discuss his academics and his progress. He sat in the overstuffed blue chair that had to be twice his age. The room smelled of musty paper, and dust could be seen floating in the sunlight that gleamed through the large window. It was winter, and the office was drafty. Quinn shivered. The professor's fireplace had only a few glowing embers and no flame.

Quickthorn took a seat behind her desk. She waved a hand in front of the fireplace, and the embers grew into a warm, glowing fire, warming the office quickly. Quinn sighed. Growing flames from embers was basic magic, and he could usually just get a spark. Although he had the Gift of the Earth, he had never progressed past the basics. He worked twice as hard in his other classes to make up for his lack of magical skill.

"Much better," the old woman said. She yawned again. "I'm sorry. I feel as if I did not sleep at all. It seems to be a trend today." Quinn nodded in agreement, wondering if she, too, had dreamed of the enveloping darkness. "Now, Mr. Atwell, your fourth year will be over in three weeks. I've noticed you have not registered an apprenticeship with me."

Quinn shifted in the armchair. At the Academy for Scholars, the students spend four years studying history, medicine, politics, and earth magic. In the fifth year, most accepted an apprenticeship in their desired fields, although some preferred to stay and conduct research or prepare for a career in teaching. "I thought I would stay and do research."

"I see. And what were you hoping to research?" Her eyes studied him, calling his bluff. She knew just as well as he did that he had not yet decided what to do.

He looked down at his lap and straightened the wrinkle in his brown linen pants. "History?" It was a question, not an answer.

"All of it?"

"Um." He searched his sleepy brain for a better answer. Last night's book popped into his mind, and he thought that would suffice for now. "The Deyoni. The history of the Deyoni." He met his professor's eyes, seeking her approval. Instead she simply arched a brow. He looked down again, ashamed. It was not for lack of trying that Quinn had no plan for his fifth year and beyond. In recent months, all he thought about was where his future lay. Medicine never intrigued him enough to pursue a career as a Healer or Apothecary. His earth magic could never be controlled, so he could not very well travel to help farmers and fishers reap great bounty. He enjoyed studying people and politics, so diplomacy intrigued him. But he lacked confidence in all new situations and failed at initiating conversations. He did not want to return to a small, backward village to teach, but he saw no other option.

After several moments of awkward silence, his professor spoke. "The other professors and I are worried. Your marks place you at the top of all the academic classes in your cohort. We haven't taught a student as bright as you in years. Additionally, you have the strongest Gift of any of the current students. Yet for some reason, you just can't control it. You're powerful, but your magic is wild. Your intuition is strong, stronger than mine. In fact, your Gift of the Earth is nearly as strong as the Sage's, I truly believe. To find you have no real plan with all your strengths is concerning."

Strongest Gift of any of the students. Quinn had to stifle a dry laugh. He had heard this before but never believed it. The Gift of the Earth is the power of Scholars. A small portion of the population was born with increased intelligence, an exceptional intuition, and most importantly, a connection to the natural world that allowed them to manipulate the elements to perform earth magic. Scholars educated at the Academy held immense power in Elandria's society. Many jobs, such as healing and diplomacy, were limited to Scholars. Quinn had always been different as a child; he could never relate to his peers, and he found his village's customs and beliefs narrow-minded by the time he reached age six. Strange things happened when he was upset: the ground would tremble or gusts of wind would knock over things. In the village, most thought he was possessed by a demon. He never believed demons existed. He learned early to stifle his emotions to avoid the uncontrollable phenomena that led the villagers of Corthy to look down on him and his family with disdain and fear.

When a Scholar came to identify children with the Gift, Quinn was the only child in Corthy to have it. He was nine years old and the first in his village with the Gift in decades. The Scholar, a gentle man with brown skin and the whitest teeth young Quinn had ever seen, told him his Gift was immensely powerful. Quinn finally had an explanation for all his peculiarity. But he was still alone. When he got to the Academy over ten years later, he was two years older than most of his classmates. He felt strange, his conservative, rural upbringing setting him apart from his peers. He had good friends, but he had always felt a bit like an outsider in the grand city of Teleah.

He excelled in his classes, that much was true. And he did have an uncanny knack for reading people and situations. But despite all the training, his earth magic remained mostly wild. While most of his peers could wave their hand over a small plot of land and grow multiple plants, he still had to hold an individual seedling just to get it to sprout. Then in bursts of his frustration, he would make a tree several feet behind him grow six inches or flood the small creek that ran through the Academy's gardens. A block, magic Professor Viridion had called it on multiple occasions. Quinn had some sort of mental block that kept him from harnessing his power.

"I don't know what career to pursue besides teaching in the rural towns." As the most educated class in Elandria, many Scholars chose to teach in small villages on the outskirts of the country. It was a noble calling, for some, but Quinn loathed the customs and ridiculous religious traditions of the outlying settlements. "I decided I should spend some more time researching before finding a teaching post after commencement."

"But is that what you want to do, Quinn?" Quickthorn asked, a motherly tone to her voice this time. She rarely called any student by their first name. Quinn felt a rush of emotion but suppressed it. He simply stared at her, unable to answer. He did not want to teach. He did not want to return to an isolated village with out-of-date customs. He certainly did not want to return home. "If you were offered the right apprenticeship, would you accept?"

"There are only three weeks until the end of the term. I don't think I'll find an apprenticeship in that time."

She smiled. "That's not what I asked. Would you accept the right apprenticeship?" Quinn nodded. It was a moot point; his peers had accepted their apprenticeships weeks ago. There was no time to apply. "Very well. I will check in with you soon." Quinn stood and turned to leave the dusty office. He turned back. He had an urge to ask his mentor something off-topic and more personal than he ever discussed.

"Professor?" She glanced at him. "I was wondering if—well, I had this strange dream last night. Except, it felt like more than a dream." She gestured at him to continue, so he sat back down in the blue chair. He described the nightmare in detail; her face was unreadable. Quickthorn took note of the slight shake in his voice as he relived the dream out loud. Quinn was normally so rational and, well, emotionless.

Finally, she spoke. "Interesting. A Scholar should always trust his intuition, and if it felt significant, then I suppose it's possible. But I am sure it was just the change in seasons that kept all of us from getting a good night's sleep." Quinn nodded, only somewhat reassured. He thanked her and left her office.

After he left, Professor Quickthorn pulled a piece of parchment from her desk drawer. She had a letter to write, an important request to make. She scribbled her message quickly. Then she paused. Quinn's power was no doubt extraordinary. She decided to include his dream, as well. It disturbed her to see this rational young man so distraught by a nightmare. She would try everything in her power to get Quinn an apprenticeship he deserved.

❦

TWO DAYS LATER, the Sage of Elandria read her mail in her study. The autumn wind grew colder, but she enjoyed the breeze blowing into the room, contrasting with the warmth of the hearth. Her large oak desk was cluttered with blank parchment, books, and a large stack of mail. Most of the correspondence was typical. A member of Parliament asked for her insight on a new law regarding taxes. A newspaper wondered if she would write them a piece in honor of the upcoming Feast of Fire. The chief Healer in a neighboring city asked for her thoughts on using the acca plant in place of melaleuca for an outbreak of skin boils. She replied to each in turn.

A letter from Prince Raymond made her laugh. He had returned from a diplomatic trip to the country of Lazoria on the northeastern border of Elandria. The Lazoris were stereotyped throughout Elandria as barbaric. He described his shock at their bathing customs: apparently, they used perfumed oils instead of soap. He called them all "stinking Lazoris" and told her he requested a gallon of soap upon his return to Elandria. He signed his letter with "all my love." She sighed. She hoped he meant it platonically, but she was not so sure.

The pile of mail grew smaller, and the Sage ached to go walk in her gardens. The broccoli should be nearly ready to harvest, and she was trying to keep her roses alive through the first chill. It was her latest earth magic experiment—shielding plants from the cold for a prolonged period. Instead she sat, stuck inside writing letters. Sometimes she loathed the mundane tasks her position required. She scribbled quick responses to each letter and sealed them with the Sage's Seal: a flaming tree with roots growing from water. Finally, just two letters remained.

She opened a letter from the king. As she read, her world slipped away. Two Scholars, traveling to identify children with the Gift of the Earth, had been slaughtered in their inn a few nights before. The king assured her it appeared to be a random crime in a small fishing town, but nothing had been stolen from their rooms.

The Sage doubted the slaughter was random. The two Scholars were killed the night of her dream, a dream that had haunted her the last few days. She clutched her Scholar's pendant. Could she simply be so connected to the earth that she can feel the murder of others with the Gift? She would have to go through the old writings of the ancient Sages. Surely, she was not the first to experience this.

Her thoughts were foggy. She uncurled her bare feet from underneath her in her chair and placed them on the cold tile, forcing herself to pull some of the magic from the earth into her mind to calm herself. A sickening grief for the lost Scholars filled the pit of her stomach. She steadied her breathing and jotted a short reply to the king. Her hands shook, and her words were few. "Keep me informed," she wrote, and sealed the letter.

The Sage wanted nothing more than to go run through her gardens and pull hope from the earth. She felt isolated; of all the Scholars who made the Sage's Villa their home, no one had dreamed the dream she did. Although, every one of them had slept poorly that night. This is no coincidence, she thought. *And I have no evidence to the contrary.* There was no one to talk to who would understand; Scholars prided themselves on their rational natures. There was nothing to do until the palace sent more information. She felt alone.

One last, unopened letter lay on her desk. She sighed. She could respond to one more letter. This one was from a former professor of hers. She always enjoyed news from the Academy and thought she would end her work on a positive note. She opened Quickthorn's letter and read.

My Lady Sage,

The other professors and I have written to you before of an exceptional student. Quinn Atwell's Gift is strong but his earth magic is untamed. He has extraordinary talent, I am sure. However, we believe only you can teach him to use his magic. We are at a loss. He has accepted no apprenticeship for his fifth year. I am writing, quite frankly, to implore you to consider taking him on as your apprentice. His intuition would serve him well as an ambassador or minister, but he lacks all confidence. I would hate to see his Gift go unused and his earth magic uncontrolled. He has the highest marks in his classes and is eager to learn. I do hope you will consider teaching him.

Today every person at the school is exhausted. Professor and student alike slept restlessly. Quinn told me he dreamed of an encroaching darkness that swallowed him whole. The way he spoke made me think it more significant than simply a nightmare. He seemed thoroughly shaken. I know we Scholars do not believe in dream magic but Quinn is far too rational to be so disturbed by a nightmare. Do you have thoughts on this?

I hope to see you soon. Your presence is missed greatly at the Academy.
All the best,
Sylvia Quickthorn

THE SAGE DROPPED THE LETTER. She had not intended to take on another apprentice for at least another year. But who was this young man who dreamed the same dream as her? Her thoughts were jumbled, and a flood of varying emotions threatened to make her scream in frustration. For what felt like the millionth time that morning, she forced her breathing to steady and wrote a response to Professor Quickthorn:

DEAR PROFESSOR QUICKTHORN,

I will accept Quinn Atwell as my apprentice for his fifth year. I will expect him a few days prior to the Feast of Fire. His apprenticeship will start on the first day of the new year.

Regards,

Amarice Teyvana, Sage of Elandria

FINISHED WITH HER CORRESPONDENCE, the Sage ran from her study, through the courtyard of her Villa, and out into the gardens. She did not stop to check her broccoli or her roses. Instead she kept running out of sight of anyone who may be outside. The damp grass felt refreshing under her bare feet. She could feel the Gift flowing from the earth through her veins. She kept running until she could barely breathe. She stopped at the blue river that flowed down Sage Mountain. She stood on the banks, splashes of icy cold water reaching her face.

She screamed as loud as she could. The river began rushing faster, and a strong gust of wind nearly knocked her over. She screamed again, trying to free herself of the ropes of emotion that bound her. The river flowed at a dangerous speed and the ground shook beneath her. Red and gold leaves flew off the trees and swirled around her in a vortex.

She sat upon the soaking banks, not bothering to create a warm energy barrier between her and the crisp wind. And the Sage of Elandria, the most powerful person to ever live, cried. She cried for the murdered Scholars. She cried for the evil that she knew crept into her peaceful country. And she cried for the loneliness that came with being the Sage.

CHAPTER 2

"What's wrong with you today?" Rafe asked over lunch. He crunched an apple loudly and waited for Quinn's reply.

Quinn had been laying with his back against a tree, eyes closed. It had been a few days since his nightmare and his meeting with Quickthorn. Between the anxiety of falling asleep and his feelings of inadequacy for disappointing his professors, Quinn had not slept much the last few days. He tried to bury himself in studying for exams, but his mind kept wandering. Although Quickthorn had assured him his dream was nothing more significant, he obsessed over it, replaying it in his mind over and over.

"I'm just nervous about exams," he replied, eyes still closed. He did not want Rafe to push the subject. While most Scholars put no stock in dreams and signs, Rafe did. His connection to the natural world was strong, and he was a master of earth magic. This made him far less grounded in empirical studies than the other Scholars. In lieu of a traditional apprenticeship, he was selected into Professor Viridion's elite group of fifth years who studied much stronger and more powerful magic than most Scholars could ever hope to possess. They were usually even invited to spend Harvest Holiday with the Sage herself so she could provide them extra guidance.

"I say that is a steaming pile of shit," Rafe retorted. "You outperform every person in every class."

"Not every class." Quinn shifted to avoid a twig digging into his thigh. He willed Rafe to drop the issue.

"Oh, get over it, Quinn. Plenty of Scholars have trouble with magic past the law of touch. So what? You can't change the direction of the wind? It's not a big deal. And the earth magic exam is entirely theory-based. You will do great at that. Now are you going to tell us what is really wrong with you?" Even with his eyes closed, Quinn knew Rafe gave him an insistent stare.

Jack piped up for the first time. "Give it up, Rafe. Most of us don't like talking about our feelings with you." His tone was sarcastic but not malicious. Quinn gave a flat laugh. He liked Jack and could always count on him to lighten the mood. He looked over at his friend with the chiseled jaw and fiery red hair. He had a collection of herbs and oils and was mixing up some sort of tincture. Despite his clownish behavior, Jack had a gift for medicine. He had accepted an apprenticeship with the oldest apothecary in Teleah. Quinn knew once his apprenticeship was over, Jack would put the old man out of business. His possessed the rare combination of exceptional talent and affable personality.

Quinn then dared to make eye contact with Rafe. Rafe was stocky with copper skin and forest green eyes. His friendly demeanor made him irresistible to the other sex—well, after the opposite sex tired of Jack's ego. "I'm fine, Rafe. Just tired." Although he often felt like a third wheel, he loved his friends. He had been lucky to end up with Rafe as his roommate in first year. Rafe never met a stranger and forced his friendship upon reserved, anxious Quinn. Quinn had grown up in what felt like the most isolated village of all the students in his year. The Gift was rare in the north; for that reason, much of the northern farm towns never adopted Elandria's progressive customs and instead clung to ancient religious traditions and morals.

Rafe did not care. He did not care that Quinn was two years older than him, as well. Rafe grew up in Teleah, the son of a merchant father and Scholar mother. His mother worked as a Healer in Teleah's hospital. His father traveled often, and his mother kept many regular lovers, most of them Scholars. He was well-versed in the Scholar culture before he ever entered the Academy. To Quinn, Rafe's life was exotic, although it was quite the norm in the cities. Marriage was uncommon in Elandria's heart, but it was expected in the villages of the north, so hearing his friend's stories of his mother's latest lover always shocked the country boy. Where Quinn grew up, earth magic was often thought of as evil and unnatural. To Rafe, it was everyday life.

First-year Rafe had been determined to bring Quinn out of his shell. He dragged him to study groups and social events. One of these parties was where Quinn met Jack. Jack's boisterous character contrasted sharply to Quinn's awkward shyness. Jack talked to Quinn the whole night then approached him at lunch the next day. Quinn had no clue why this popular young man wanted to be friends, but he was so desperate to be accepted by his peers that he began eating lunch with him every day.

After a few weeks, Jack had made his intentions clear: he was desperately trying to bed Quinn. Quinn was shocked; men sleeping with men was unheard of in his home town, and he had not yet adopted Teleah's romantic culture. He politely expressed his lack of interest in men, but he could not contain his shock. Jack found Quinn's naivete endearing, and they remained good friends.

"Well, I'm still not convinced, but I'll leave it alone until you're ready to talk," Rafe relented. I won't be ready to talk, Quinn thought. Jack just rolled his eyes. In truth, Quinn appreciated how much Rafe cared. His roommate had become not only his friend, but the closest feeling to a family he had ever experienced. It was not Rafe's fault that Quinn was so guarded. Rafe changed the subject, "Did you read the newspaper today?" His friends shook their heads. "Two Scholars were murdered at an inn a few nights ago."

Quinn sat up abruptly and clutched his pendant. Jack stopped messing with his tincture. With his flair for the dramatic, Rafe relayed the story: two Scholars were staying in a fishing village, scouting for the Gift among the local children. Their throats were slit in their sleep. There was no sign of burglary.

This sort of news story was wildly out-of-place in Elandria. Murders were rare, and nearly always the result of a domestic dispute or a robbery gone wrong. Murders of Scholars simply did not happen. Scholars were respected throughout Elandria. Their status was immediately recognized by their Scholar's pendant: a golden medallion depicting a tree of knowledge inside a diamond, the four points representing the four elements of nature. "The Royal Inquisitors have ruled it a random attack. They have not found the murderer, though."

"When did this happen?" Quinn asked. He felt he knew the answer.

"Three—no, four nights ago." Quinn felt his breath leave him; he paled. "What's wrong?" Rafe asked, puzzled by Quinn's reaction.

"That was the night... the night we all slept terribly." Quinn's heart pounded in his chest. Did he dream that two Scholars were murdered? Surely he did not. No one had that sort of psychic ability.

"Was it?" Rafe mused. "Strange." Overall, he appeared unconcerned. He changed the subject again. "Hey, Quinn. Sarah's looking at you."

"What?" Quinn placed his hands on the ground, forcing himself to draw calm from the earth. "Oh, Sarah. Right." Sarah was a pretty girl, tall with long, blonde hair. She had expressed an interest in Quinn for years. She had dated both Rafe and Jack, but her flirting with Quinn never ceased. She was smart and kind, but Quinn never pursued her. He had no clue how to date women from Teleah. And he certainly had no interest at this moment. He waved at her half-heartedly across the courtyard. Sarah sat with a large group of girls under an ancient oak. She flashed him a coy smile and giggled with her friends. Why his awkwardness was so endearing, he would never understand.

He studied the rest of the courtyard. The ivy lining the ancient stone buildings had faded. The leaves had changed to autumn colors, and the grass was dry and brown. The fourth-year students were easily identified by their intense studying. Other groups of students chatted happily. He looked over at a loud, laughing group of second-year students. In a concerted effort, they revitalized individual blades of grass to be alive and green once more. Quinn strained his neck to see what they were spelling. The green, grassy letters "F... U... C..." stood out on the dead ground. The young students laughed harder as they completed their "K." He shook his head. He wished he could use earth magic for something as light-hearted as spelling obscenities on the grounds of the ancient Academy.

His thoughts refocused on his nightmare. Ever the rationalist, he mentally listed all the reasons it was a coincidence. He did not convince himself, but his heart stopped racing. The sudden appearance of Professor Quickthorn forced him back into reality. "Mr. Atwell, would you walk with me?" She held a letter in her hand. Quinn greeted her and scrambled to his feet, dusting the dirt off his black cotton pants.

⚜

QUINN FOLLOWED the old Scholar toward her office once again. He hoped she had asked around and had information about his dream, but he thought it was unlikely. She probably wanted to know if he had given any more thought to his research.

Quickthorn gestured for him to enter her office. She handed him the letter in her hand and shut the door behind them. "Read it," she insisted. He gave her a confused look, then read the letter.

Then he read it again. And again. "I'm confused."

Professor Quickthorn laughed from her desk chair. "Confused? My dear boy, I thought the letter quite succinct. You have been offered an apprenticeship from the Sage of Elandria."

"But—I—how?" He felt certain this was a mistake.

"The Sage only accepts apprentices with the strongest Gift. They must come highly recommended by the professors. We feel that the Sage can help you harness your magic and hopefully give your life some direction." She gave him a warm smile, making her wrinkled eyes seem even older. "Will you accept?"

Quinn stood speechless. He had barely stepped from the doorway which now felt awkward. He nodded and made his way to the blue armchair. He could not help but feel this was a mistake. An apprenticeship with the Sage seemed much more fitting for someone like Rafe.

The Sage was always the most powerful Scholar of the day. With only two exceptions in the last thousand years, the Sage was always a woman. She served as the forefront of the Scholar community, the reigning expert on all issues of earth magic, medicine, and culture, and acted as the closest advisor of the royal family. Whoever apprenticed with the Sage went on to become powerful magic practitioners, professors, important diplomats, and gifted healers. Quinn had always understood that her apprentices were the best and most powerful student Scholars. True, his marks were impressive in every class he took. But what about that mental block Professor Viridion always mentioned?

"I think you will like the Lady Sage. She is warm and pleasant. And the Villa—well, it's every Scholar's dream. The connection to the earth is incredible. You may never want to leave." She smiled again. "You should feel proud of yourself, Mr. Atwell. I will arrange for a school carriage to take you to the Villa two days before the Feast of Fire. Now, if you'll excuse me, I've got a meeting with a third-year student who has decided to fail my class." Quinn thanked her and handed her back the letter. She waved her hand. "Keep it. It may be addressed to me, but it belongs to you."

QUINN LEFT the dark corridor of offices and re-entered the bright courtyard. For the first time in days, he appreciated the changing colors of the leaves and the crisp air. For the first time in days, he let himself smile.

He joined Rafe and Jack. Rafe had his nose in a history book, which had always been his worst subject. Jack muttered obscenities over his herbs as he ground them in his mortar and pestle. Apparently, he could not perfect this latest solution. Quinn grabbed an apple from his bag and sat down cross-legged under the poplar tree.

Rafe peered at Quinn over the top of his book. "What did Quickthorn want this time?" Quinn laughed and handed his best friend the letter. Rafe read it. "Brigitte's tit!" he exclaimed, a fitting swear in honor of the first Sage. "I didn't know you had applied for that!" Jack was interested again and grabbed the letter from Rafe. He looked at Quinn in amazement.

"I didn't either," Quinn told them. "Apparently, it's all professor recommendation. I had no clue." He chewed his apple, which he swore tasted as if it were the sweetest apple ever to fall from a tree.

"We've got to celebrate!" Rafe exclaimed. "Jack, put your damn herbs away. We're going to Bucky's." Quinn protested half-heartedly, citing their need to study. "No, gallons of ale await us." And the three friends left their studies to visit their favorite tavern.

※

BY THE TIME the trio stumbled back to their dorms that night, Quinn was well and truly drunk. He felt happy and content. He collapsed into bed without undressing and fell to sleep as soon as his head hit the pillow.

Tonight, he dreamed of bright, vivid colors swirling and rich melodies floating through the air. A great darkness approached the colors. The music stopped abruptly. A final screech of a horn sounded, and the darkness swallowed the colors until there was a great nothingness.

Quinn did not wake, but he recalled the dream in the morning. He pushed his feelings of fear aside because he was far too happy to care. He blamed the copious amounts of Bucky's strongest brew for the nightmare and went about his studies.

※

AT THE VILLA, the Sage puzzled over this latest dream. If only there were someone she could ask for counsel. Unfortunately, the Sage was the counsel. She scoured her books and the records left by previous Sages. The only time a Sage recorded a strange dream had been three hundred years ago, just before the great Deyoni rebellion had begun.

※

OUTSIDE OF THE Great Northern Forest, a small band of Deyoni had made camp. Their silken tents and painted wagons shone brightly in the moonlight against the dark background of the ancient forest. They had returned to camp at the foot of the forest after their successful venture in a nearby village. Their dancing and fire-breathing had earned them enough money to last through the end of the year. Tonight, they had celebrated.

Their fire burned, untended. Twenty Deyoni—men, women, and children—lay dead on the ground. A group of strangers had approached in the darkness, wielding swords and axes. The Deyoni had been forbidden for carrying weapons for the last three centuries. On this night, they had no chance of survival.

CHAPTER 3

"I've heard she's the most beautiful woman in the world."

Quinn sighed, ignoring Rafe, and continued folding his clothes to place in his trunk. Ever since he had received word that the Sage would take him as an apprentice, his friends could talk of nothing but the mysterious woman. That would be fine, he thought, if they cared why she was the Sage. At least Rafe had a bit more decorum when he spoke of the most powerful person in all Elandria. Jack had become increasingly obscene with his fantasies of the Sage.

"I've heard her parties are wild. When she starts dancing, people just start fucking each other, like a spell." Jack lay reclined on the cobbled floor between Quinn and Rafe's beds, determined to be obnoxious and in the way while Quinn packed.

Quinn rolled his eyes. "It's not a spell. There are no such things as spells. You're a Scholar. You should know that. And we've been to plenty of parties where people dance and fuck each other. In fact, isn't that what most parties in Elandria are?" He placed his neatly folded pants in his trunk.

"Not for you, they're not," Jack countered. "I bet the Sage is amazing in bed. Not that it matters for you, Quinn. We all know ladies aren't really your thing."

Quinn threw a freshly laundered linen shirt at his redheaded philanderer of a friend. Just because he didn't screw everything with breasts did not mean he was uninterested. He may be far from home, but the liberated culture in Teleah still felt taboo. Four years in the city had not been enough to break him of years of indoctrination. Four years with Jack as a friend had not been enough.

"I'm joking. If you preferred men, you wouldn't have turned me down in first year." Jack threw back Quinn's shirt, then took a swig of whiskey from his flask. "It's not fair though. You are going to apprentice with the sexiest woman in the world, and you don't even appreciate it."

"I appreciate it plenty. I appreciate that I'm going to study with the most intelligent Scholar that ever lived. I appreciate that I'm going to learn her magic. I appreciate that she's going to teach me about people and nature and politics and medicine." He packed away the rest of his clothes and began to gather the last of his belongings that made their home on his desk.

His friends groaned. He knew they were jealous as Scholars, though, and not just as young men with high sex drives. He packed his books, noticing how many of the titles were written by the current Sage. In less than twenty-four hours, he could discuss her work with the Scholar herself.

He remembered the first book of hers he ever read at the young age of fourteen. By that time, he had read every work of every Sage and Scholar that his tiny village library held. The librarian handed him the brand-new book, written by a first-year Scholar student. It was deeper, more insightful than any other work he had read. But it was also fun to read. Scholar works tended to be dry like encyclopedias. But Taboos in Earth Magic was witty and vibrant. He read it in one night, then he read it again the next day.

The girl wrote three more books that year. Quinn was amazed when he learned these brilliant works were written by a sixteen-year-old. Her gift had been identified by an early teacher, and she left for the city two years earlier than most with the Gift. And news began to travel about a young girl who with the strongest Gift anyone had seen. Her earth magic was second to no one, living or dead. She brought an amazing insight into healing and medicine that she had taught herself as a young girl. Her intuition for reading people was unsettling. She completed four years of study in only two, and she went to apprentice with the Sage of the time.

After only three months, the current Sage, Marietta, shocked the country when she said she had nothing more to teach the girl. She had taught her the politics required of the Sage, but the girl's power exceeded her own. The middle-aged woman publicly stated that she could no longer call herself Sage when the Gift was so strong in another. Most Sages held their position until they died, and on their death beds would select as Sage the Scholar who demonstrated the greatest power. But Marietta retired to a mansion by the sea, and a girl named Amarice became Sage at the age of eighteen, the youngest and most powerful ever.

That was eight years ago, when Quinn was just sixteen. In those eight years, Quinn had read every book, article, and pamphlet the Sage had ever written. He admired her intelligence and wit. It took him several more years to get to the Academy for Scholars in the capital city. Most people never left his tiny northern village of Corthy, and he had to work hard to pay for the journey. He was only two years older than most of the students in his year, but his rural upbringing often had him feeling years younger.

He had wanted to be a Scholar since he was a small boy. Once his Gift was identified, his sole purpose in life became finding his way to Teleah to study at the Academy. He had hoped he could at least hear the Sage speak once in his life. He never dreamed he would be packing his trunk to move to her Villa.

As his peers prepared for either another year of study or various apprenticeships in the city, Quinn prepared to move to the lush, green Sage Mountains outside the city to study under his idol. The shock had not yet worn off; a large part of Quinn still believed his apprenticeship had been a mistake.

"... and then we'll go to Bucky's Tavern. Is that good, Quinn?" Rafe's voice snapped him back to reality. His best friends had organized a farewell party in his honor.

"Bucky's. Yeah, that's great."

"You heard nothing else I said, did you? Dinner in town, a party in the square, then Bucky's. And Sarah will be there. She's devastated you're leaving. Here, start drinking." Rafe handed him the flask. He knew Quinn well enough that any mention of a woman interested in his friend would have him nervous and withdrawn. Liquor fixed that, usually, and kept Quinn laughing. Just once, though, he would have liked to see Quinn leave his anxious mind and live in the moment.

Quinn took a large drink of the whiskey, enjoying the burn on his throat. He liked Sarah; he would be stupid not to like her. She was gorgeous, and smart, and funny. But he did not know if he connected enough to give her what she wanted; he certainly did not love her. It did not matter anymore. He was going away tomorrow for an indeterminate amount of time, and she would begin apprenticing at the local hospital. He decided not to fret about it. He was going to get drunk with his friends on his last night in the city. Tomorrow was a new chapter.

◈◈◈

QUINN TOOK care to notice all the details of the city where he had made his home the last four years. He stayed quiet, absorbing the moment, while Rafe and Jack laughed and hollered behind him. They had already drunk much more than Quinn, as usual.

As dusk fell, and the lamplighters illuminated the cobblestone streets, Quinn smiled. Although he had grown up on a farm in the northern moorlands, he had grown to love Teleah with all its character and life. Narrow wooden buildings, often painted in bright colors, wedged next to stone architecture colored with history. Shop owners and patrons alike were typically friendly, in stark contrast to the cold, gossipy villagers of Quinn's youth. The Scholars' presence was undeniable: every two or three blocks, luscious gardens and green spaces abounded for all residents of Teleah to enjoy. Over all the busy streets, the palace rested on a hilltop. White stone glistened in the sunset, a beacon of the centuries-long peace that kept all the people of Elandria safe and content. Till recently, Quinn thought bitterly.

The narrow streets near the ancient Academy were busy tonight.

Teleans bundled up against the wind in cloaks. Peppered in the crowd of the citizens were more students than usual for a weeknight. The school year ended with a full week before the new year, so the students had created their own unofficial holiday week. Few students returned home between terms, choosing instead to stay in the capital to drink, party, recover, and do it all again the next night. Barkeeps worked overtime, but by the Feast of Fire that marked the year's end, their safes were filled with extra coin.

They passed a large, open recreation area. Campfires burned among tents of brightly colored fabric. At least a hundred Deyoni had sat up camp here. It was strange; the nomadic tribes usually balked at city life, preferring instead the open lands where they encountered fewer prejudiced Elandrians. They had a reputation for being thieves and charlatans; even most Scholars viewed them with a certain arrogant disdain. Quinn inquired from his friends as to their presence in the park.

Rafe informed him Teleah and the other major cities were seeing an influx of Deyoni. After the unexplained slaughter of a small tribe, the nomads felt unsafe. Many in the outlying areas had used the attack as a reason to turn violent toward other Deyoni tribes. The cities held much stronger pro-Deyoni laws, thanks in large part to the work of the young Sage. She had used much of her political influence to help end legal discrimination against the culture, but she had not managed to convince the Parliament to overturn the three-hundred-year weapons ban. Unable to protect themselves, they headed for the safety of the cities.

Rafe always viewed the Deyoni with respect. Quinn simply felt curious. Once, when he was a boy, a large tribe had set up a carnival near his village. His parents would not let him go see the legendary shows and dances, citing the sinful nature of their beliefs. He recalled his mother, in general a passive woman, yelling at his younger self for his perpetual nag to go. Her uncharacteristic outburst shut the boy up quickly. The Deyoni did not stay long, because every shopkeeper in Corthy refused to sell them so much as a loaf of bread.

A block past the Deyoni's impromptu camp, smells of roasted meats drifted onto the street from a small wooden building. The young men entered the cozy, low-light establishment. A few more of the trio's cohort joined them for dinner in Quinn's favorite restaurant. Sarah had traded her typical cotton pants and tunic for a fitted dress of thin, blue silk. It revealed much of her back and shoulders, where her normally braided blonde hair cascaded. Quinn could not help but think she must be cold; the height of winter was upon them, and though Teleah was relatively temperate, Quinn had opted for leather pants and a heavy tunic to beat the chill. Once the alcohol took effect, the student Scholars would be unable to use their magic to keep themselves warm. Sarah sat herself next to Quinn at the restaurant, laughing at every word that came out of his mouth and placing a hand on him at every chance she got. He grew increasingly uncomfortable, and in response, drank copious amounts of sweet mead.

With their bellies full of warm food and good libations, the rambunctious crowd ambled toward the square. Every night of the last week of the year boasted a party of young student Scholars. Musically inclined peers played their instruments, while the rest danced, laughed, and passed bottles of whiskey and wine through the crowd.

Normally Quinn found the parties too loud and crowded. Tonight, he felt the rhythm of the drums in his blood, swaying without a care. He laughed with Rafe about Jack's shameless dancing. He watched the girls dance and even smiled when Sarah eyed him seductively. His head grew cloudy with drink, and the swaying turned into spinning.

He found a seat on a stone bench to regain his senses. Two younger students were intertwined on the other end of the bench, not at all discreet with their passion for one another. This was the norm at parties in the capital; soon couples would run off and hide behind trees or in partially abandoned alleys. Quinn laughed aloud at the memory of the first time he caught Rafe with a girl; he had wandered around the streets and heard his roommate's voice from the alley behind a bar. Worried he was in danger, Quinn had drunkenly staggered to save his friend, only to find him in the middle of making love to the barmaid he had met earlier that evening. Quinn had stood there, awkwardly apologizing until Rafe yelled at him to go away.

The couple on the bench stopped kissing at the sound of Quinn's laughter. They shot him a rude glance, assuming he had laughed at them, before disappearing into the crowd. Quinn stretched his tall frame out across the cold bench, enjoying the drums and winter breeze. He may never have fully felt a part of Teleah, but he would miss this city.

☙❧

AFTER SOME TIME, Rafe found Quinn and yelled in his ear that they should head toward Bucky's Tavern. Quinn stumbled behind him, his ears still pounding with the noise of the drums even three blocks away. His horde of friends followed raucously. Jack sang offensive songs at the top of his lungs, swaying in the dark, with a girl he had just met on his arm.

Bucky's was already crowded by the time the crew arrived. Despite his busy establishment, Bucky greeted Quinn with a cheerful bellow. The trio had spent many hours here, and the tall, chocolate-skinned barkeep had grown attached to his favorite young patrons. He assured Quinn with a toothy grin that everything he drank tonight would not cost him a dime.

The bar was warm and bright. Bucky had placed mirrors around the wooden walls to reflect the light of the oil lamps. Often when Quinn and his friends left the tavern, they were shocked to discover it was still dark outside because Bucky's always felt thoroughly alive. Quinn once realized it was a genius business model: make guests forget how late it is, and they will just keep drinking.

The group recounted their favorite memories of the last four years at the Academy. Even though only Quinn would leave the capital tomorrow, their various apprenticeships guaranteed much less socializing in the year to come. And in a year, they would start careers of their own all over the country.

The night wore on. Jack disappeared with the young woman from earlier and a handsome second-year boy. Rafe had attempted to challenge every person in the tavern to a drinking game, but everyone just laughed at his slurred speech and sloppy grin. A visiting minstrel played a fast-paced ballad on his stringed instrument. Rafe, having lost all sense of decorum several pints previously, climbed on a table and began to dance. Cheered on by the crowd, he made a fool of himself, relishing the attention.

Quinn watched his friend from the back wall, smiling. Sarah sidled up to him and slipped her arm around his waist. She smelled good, like roses and honey. His heart pounded in his chest; he worried she would hear it. "Rafe is ridiculous when he's drunk," Sarah commented. "He basically becomes Jack. Well, sober Jack. Drunk Jack becomes a whore." Quinn nodded and sipped his ale.

Put your arm around her, he told himself. He unfroze and placed his hand on the small of her back. Her silk dress was hardly a barrier between his hand and her skin. He no longer cared what Rafe was doing, but he felt unsure what to do next. He looked down at the blonde woman next to him; though she was tall, he still towered over her.

Sarah reached up and stroked Quinn's neatly parted brown hair. "You're so shy," she murmured. His breathing quickened in anticipation. "I'm going to kiss you, all right?" He nodded, and she stretched to meet his lips with hers.

She kissed him forcefully, and, he could not help but notice, a bit sloppily. But she smelled good, so he returned the kiss. His head was thick with drink and desire. When she broke away, she took his hand and led him through the crowd and up the tavern stairs to the few rooms Bucky leased. Quinn followed, studying the curve of her hips and the pale skin of her back. Upstairs, Sarah fumbled with the lock on a narrow wooden door. It was quieter up here, but Quinn could still hear the raucous laughter from below. "I reserved a room earlier today before they were all taken," she told him. "I was hoping you would let me give you a farewell gift." She shot him a sensual glance as she unlocked the door.

They entered the small bedroom. Quinn stayed near the door. The moonlight illuminated Sarah through the open window. She unhooked the straps of her dress and let the silk fall from her naked body. Quinn stared, aroused but unsure what to do next. "I like you, Quinn," she told him.

Quinn cleared his throat. "I like you, too. Really." He shifted his weight.

Sarah sighed. "I have wanted you for a long time, and this is your last night in the city. Don't make me beg."

Quinn stared at the beautiful blonde in front of him. He was a long way from his old-fashioned village and their shameful concepts of sin. Tomorrow, he left Teleah for his apprenticeship. It was time he acted like he had lived in the capital. Sarah was attractive and pleasant. He downed the rest of his ale in a large gulp and threw the mug aside. "Why the hell not?" he said. And he crossed the room and pulled her into bed.

CHAPTER 4

The sun hit Quinn's face as if someone had dropped bricks on him. He groaned and turned to look at the clock, but it was not next to his nightstand. As he gathered his senses, he realized he was in a bed in Bucky's Tavern, and Sarah lay next him. He groaned again as he sat up to find the clock. His head pounded like the drummers from the square had taken up residence behind his eyes. He searched the dated room with its warped wood-paneled walls for the time.

Five minutes till seven. "FUCK!" he exclaimed. Sarah bolted upright, sleep and confusion mixing on her face. "I have to go. I'm being picked up from the dorms at half-past eight." He fumbled for his clothes, trying to ignore the pain in his skull. He kept the bedsheet wrapped around his waist, his normal inhibitions returning.

Sarah sat, clutching the faded quilt to her chest. She stared at him, hurt that he seemed to pay her no mind. This was not the morning she had imagined for the last four years. Nor was last night what she had imagined. She watched him pull the tunic over his head. Once dressed, he finally seemed to notice her. "I'm sorry," he told her. "I need to go back and change and get my trunk downstairs." She only nodded.

Quinn smiled a bit, but using the muscles in his face hurt. "Last night was... I mean, was last night--?"

"Yeah," she replied, with a contrived nonchalance. "It was all right, but you know, we were both drunk..."

"Well, good. I need to go. I'll write to you." Sarah forced a half-hearted smile at Quinn, who turned and walked out the door.

He fumbled down the stairs, head aching and stomach churning from a night of overindulgence. The sun blinded him as he opened the door onto the cobblestone street. He turned and vomited into a bush next to the tavern's red door before rushing back to the school. He felt like shit, and he was supposed to meet the Sage today.

He walked as fast as his hangover would allow him. Thankfully, Bucky's Tavern was just a few blocks from the Academy. As he approached, he tried to appreciate the beauty of the ancient stone buildings that comprised the headquarters for all Scholars. He would not be returning for some time, and he would never again call the school his home. He tried, but he felt too sick to care.

The air was still today, and warmer than it had been the last few weeks. Winters in Elandria were mild, and snow never fell in this region. In fact, Quinn had never once seen snow. He loved the cold, and he always imagined he would enjoy seeing fluffy white ice falling on mountains. A few birds chirped, appreciative of the higher temperatures, and Quinn wished they would not make so much noise. He had to pull himself together, and he hoped he would see Jack this morning for his famous hangover cure.

Quinn crossed under the large stone arch that marked the threshold of the campus and made a quick right to his dormitory, one of the "new" buildings built five hundred years ago, when the Academy had expanded. A few other students who had not slept in their own beds made their way to various dorm buildings; otherwise, the campus was quiet. Except for those damn birds who had no respect for hungover student Scholars. He pushed open the heavy, wooden door of his building and willed himself to climb the six flights of stairs to his room. A petite girl he recognized as a second-year left Quinn's dorm as he approached. She grinned at him and flounced down the staircase.

"He returns!" Rafe proclaimed proudly as Quinn entered the drafty room. Jack grumbled from Quinn's bed; apparently, he never made it to his own room down the hall last night. "Jack, wake up," Rafe pressed. "Our boy has returned a man."

"Please be quiet," Quinn pleaded, rubbing his head.

Rafe laughed. "Rough night? I've never seen you so drunk. You look disgusting. Go, bathe. I'll wake Jack up to brew us some of his tea." He threw a fresh pair of clothes at Quinn. Somehow, Rafe could drink copious amounts and never feel the least bit sick the next day. And he was so damn chipper upon waking; it was always annoying, but Quinn thought he might in fact miss his friend's bright demeanor in the mornings.

Quinn climbed back down the stairs, eager for a cold bath. He entered the open, tiled room with baths fed by an aqueduct. He did not have long to linger, but he would enjoy what he could. The baths were empty of other students. Most people used the public baths, which were larger with more variety in temperature and fragrances, but Quinn had always used the baths in the dormitory. Back in his farming village, bathing was done privately with a pitcher of hot water. Quinn smiled as he remembered the first time Rafe and some others struck up a conversation with him as he had quickly lathered himself with soap. Elandria's city-folk loved both hygiene and recreation, and baths were a perfect combination of the two.

He plunged his whole body into the cold pool, shocking himself back into sobriety. The cool water lapped over his skin, washing away the smell of alcohol and smoke from the tavern's hearth. His head broke the surface, and he selected a chunk of sandalwood soap from the side of the pool. He scrubbed himself head to toe, until his pale skin turned pink. His head still throbbed, but he felt far more human than he had before.

He stood near the fireplace as he dried himself, then dressed into the typical linen attire of a short tunic and breeches that Scholars wore, before returning upstairs to his room. Jack shoved a cup of his hangover tea into Quinn's hand, and Rafe handed him a piece of flaky bread with jam. Jack's tea tasted warm and delicious, an herbaceous blend that Quinn could not identify. With a gift for herbs and medicine from the start, Jack had spent two years perfecting his brew. It treated headaches and sour stomachs, while also removing the sleepiness that follows from a night of heavy drinking. He refused to give anyone the recipe and sold it to other students for extra money. Only Rafe and Quinn were lucky enough to have a free supply, but even they were not privy to Jack's secret brew.

Quinn leaned back in his rickety desk chair, and his friends studied him eagerly as he downed the tea. The second he finished, the pain in his head already easing, Rafe broke the silence. "Well, kid, you finally did it. How was it?" At last sober enough to think, Quinn tried to piece together last night's foggy events. He remembered Sarah's face this morning and felt a twinge of regret.

"Fine." He chewed a bite of bread. He hoped they would not press the matter.

His friends groaned. "Fine? We've been waiting four years for you to lose your virginity, and all we get is fine?!?" Rafe chided.

"There's not much to tell. And Sarah wasn't my first."

Jack groaned. "Oh, yes. The mystical farm girl of your youth. Well, considering you have lived the last four years as a celibate, last night was important to us." Rafe chortled.

Quinn's mind wandered back the farm girl he had loved. Elaine. He had known her his whole life, the only girl who never treated him differently because of his Gift. She was kind, with pale blue eyes and sun-streaked hair. She was mild-mannered, and friendly, though not very bright. She would simply nod as Quinn rambled on about the things he read, the life he wanted to live as a Scholar. She never challenged his views, never reprimanded him for questioning the status quo of the village. She loved him despite his rejection of the local religion and his refusal to accept things the way they were. As they grew older, they courted. Their parents approved; Quinn's mother desperately hoped a good marriage would make her strange son more normal. He tried so hard to convince Elaine to come to the capital with him. She remained noncommittal, hoping, he knew, that he would decide to stay with her instead.

The night before Harvest Day, the young couple had once again sneaked away to a small wooded area to kiss, far from watchful, prudish eyes. With the whole town preparing for the largest feast of the year, they had more time than usual to spend together. Their kisses grew more heated, and Elaine had led his hand to the buttons of her stiff, cotton dress. They made love in the trees, and to Quinn it was perfect. He knew Elaine would accept a ring and a marriage proposal for her Harvest Day gift the next day, and then she would come with him to Teleah, where she would keep house while he studied to become a Scholar.

The next morning, at the village's Harvest Day worship service, Quinn was all smiles. He did not even mind the ridiculous prayers of thanks to their imaginary gods. His smile vanished as Elaine walked, shaking, to the front of the church. There, in front of the entire village, she confessed her sin of sexual impurity. She did not name Quinn, but there was no need. Everyone turned to face him. He sat on the wooden bench, shocked and betrayed. It was only then that he realized his love for her could not overcome the fact that he did not belong. If he needed further proof that he was an outcast, his anger resulted in a ferocious rumbling of the ground, a wild magic earthquake. The walls of the church shook and people cried out in fear. He forced himself to stifle his emotions as he walked out of the building.

His parents would not speak to him at the village picnic. Elaine avoided him. He overheard an elder tell his mother that Quinn's rebellious nature was not her fault. His mother only smiled sadly. The shopkeeper who employed Quinn was the only person, besides his twelve-year-old brother, who spoke to Quinn that day. He informed Quinn he would no longer be employed after the weeklong Harvest Holiday's celebrations ended.

That night, Quinn packed a bag quietly with the money he had saved, his books, and a few clothes. He whispered goodbye to his sleeping brother and left. He did not belong there, and he would not curse his family with his continued presence. He was miles away by the time the sun rose. No businesses were open and he could not hire a ride to the capital until the week of Harvest Holiday celebrations were over. He slept on the side of the road until he found a merchant willing to take him along to Teleah. Once there, he had three weeks to live on his own before the new term began at the Academy. He found a friendly tavern near the school, with a jolly barkeep name Bucky.

Quinn traded Elaine's engagement ring for lodging. Then the day after the Feast of Fire, he began his new life as a student Scholar.

He suppressed the wave of emotion, his best talent, and returned his thoughts to his friends. They were used to Quinn getting lost in his own head. He forced a smile. "Yes, it was fine," he told them again.

"How was Sarah this morning?" Rafe inquired.

Quinn averted his eyes in shame. "I don't really know. I had to rush back here. I overslept." He focused on chewing the rest of his food, willing his friends to drop the issue. But Rafe never dropped the issue.

"Did you at least kiss her goodbye?" Quinn stared blankly. His friends exclaimed at his stupidity and rudeness, but Rafe stopped when he noticed Quinn's face full of shame. "It's all right, Quinn. Sarah's used to one-night lovers. Come on, let's get your stuff downstairs. The carriage will be here soon."

His friends helped him carry his trunk down the six flights of narrow stairs and out to the front of the school. They waited with him by the stone arch that marked the entrance to the Academy. Jack presented him with a large supply of hangover tea, "for all the parties at the Villa," he told him. He gave Quinn a friendly hug.

Rafe presented his friend with a leather-bound journal. On the front, in gold lettering, he had had Quinn's name embossed. On the first page, Rafe's scrawling handwriting read, "For all the things you learn and the stories you have to tell. The world needs to hear the voice of Quinn Atwell." Quinn was speechless at the thoughtful gift. He swallowed hard and wrapped his best friend in a warm embrace. He would miss the Academy, the city, and his friends. But he would miss Rafe most of all.

The trio chatted until the carriage arrived, the Scholar's symbol painted on the side. They helped him load his trunk and said their farewells once more. Quinn climbed inside the carriage and waved, then settled in for the six-hour ride to the Sage's Villa to begin his apprenticeship.

CHAPTER 5

The carriage passed through the city gates, taking Quinn out of Teleah for the first time in four years. Through the open carriage window, the amalgamation of city odors shifted to a light scent of pure, open country. He watched as the scenery changed from modest houses near their neighbors to wide swaths of harvested farmland. The capital was nestled in a valley, surrounded by some of the largest farms in the country. To the west ran the River Nyva, the source of the capital's massive aqueduct network. The region was bounded on the south by the start of the southern moorlands and to the east, the Scholars' Forest. But this carriage traveled north to the low mountain range overlooking the valley.

The Sage Mountains had been home to every Sage for a thousand years. Legend said the heart of the earth lay in the soft green slopes of these mountains. A thousand years ago, the Gift of the Earth was far more prevalent than it was today, with most of the population able to control the elements to a degree. Before there were large cities and massive trade networks, the people here lived as one with the earth. Over time, however, tension between the settlers in the valley and the Deyoni tribes escalated into large-scale violence. The most powerful of the settlers, Brigitte, used her power to help run off the Deyoni.

After the war, Brigitte refused the offer of leadership. She wished to live out her days in peace with the earth, racked with guilt for using the Gift for non-peaceful ends. Leadership passed by unanimous agreement to the greatest of the war heroes, Torith, establishing the royal bloodline. Torith loved Brigitte and asked for her hand in marriage. Though she loved him, she refused again, retreating to the nearby mountains. As Torith began building the city of Teleah, he also built her a grand residence. He sought her council through the rest of his reign, setting the precedent for the role of Sage as the royal family's closest advisor. She counseled him to be a peaceful ruler and to listen to his people. When Torith's daughter became Queen after his death, Brigitte helped her establish the Royal Parliament, the first ever popularly elected body of leadership the world had ever seen. She died, passing on the title of Sage to a powerful woman, Magda, who established the Academy for Scholars.

Quinn mused on this history as he studied the camps of Deyoni set up along the side of the road. Attacks on the Deyoni had increased, as if the first slaughter was somehow permission for rural villagers to act on their bigotry. How ironic, he thought, that they return to the valley for protection when they had been forced out a millennium before. Their tents were made of skins and bright, summer-colored silks contrasted with the autumn shades of the landscape. The smell of roasting meat from their fires mingled in the cool breeze. Many stood watching the carriages that passed on the busy Royal Road, their dark eyes touched with a note of fear.

The hours passed, and the camps of Deyoni tribes transitioned into more open farmland filled with herds of sheep and cattle out to graze. Quinn dozed on and off, exhausted from the night before. How he wished he had returned for a night of decent sleep in his own bed. How he wished he had not left Sarah with a look of hurt on her face. Perhaps he should write her a letter of apology. Or perhaps it was best that she remained angry with him, so he did not give her false hope of a future he did not want.

Around midday, the carriage stopped alongside a small babbling creek at the foot of the Sage Mountains. The driver offered Quinn some of his roast chicken, and they ate on the banks of the creek while the chestnut horse drank and rested. "Just a couple hours now," the driver informed Quinn. "Have you met the Sage before?" Quinn shook his head no. "Nice lady," the driver offered. "And the prettiest lady I've ever seen; just don't tell my wife."

Quinn laughed politely. He wondered if the driver understood the immense power that this Sage had. The history books had always described Brigitte as having abilities no other with the Gift could possess. From her first year at the Academy, Amarice had been described by the professors as far more powerful than Brigitte had been. Some said she could control the weather and reroute whole rivers. And she was far more involved in politics than her ancient predecessor. Amarice worked tirelessly for increased rights for the Deyoni. Rumors abounded. Some said Amarice was a descendant of Brigitte's, though Amarice had never confirmed this. Among the common people, many believed that the current Sage was Brigitte, returned to make amends for her acts against the Deyoni. In the rural outskirts of Elandria, the Sage was always viewed with a sense of fear, and the word "sorceress" regularly passed the lips of those that clung to dated religions.

After their brief lunch, the carriage began its ascent up the mountain road. The air grew warmer, despite the change in elevation. Here, the grass was still a pale green and only half the trees had changed to red and gold, as if winter had barely touched the land on these mountains. Their pace slowed, and they passed no other carriages or riders for the remainder of the journey. Quinn embraced the peace; for all his love of the capital, he had been born in the quiet countryside and reveled in the stillness that can come only outside of densely populated towns and cities.

The carriage trotted up the mountain for another few hours. Quinn had grown so accustomed to the relaxing pace with the sweet mountain air blowing through the window that he was quite shocked by carriage's abrupt stop. He looked out the window and could see only a lush garden overlooked by the higher mountain peaks in the distance. The driver came around and opened the door. "We've arrived, sir."

The young apprentice stepped out of the carriage into the bright sunlight and stretched. He ached; carriages were not designed for people of his height. He turned to the north and caught his first glimpse of the Sage's Villa. He could not stifle his gasp. "Beautiful, eh?" the driver asked.

But beautiful did not begin to describe it. The Villa seemed to grow directly out of the mountain, a glistening white stone building surrounded by the most vibrant gardens Quinn had ever seen. Winter plants and evergreen trees lined stone walkways. The sunlight glinted off the massive structure, which sat framed by a cerulean sky as if it had always been there. Layers of emerald-toned ivy wound along parts of the white walls. Only two stories high, the Villa's vastness made it the largest individual building Quinn had seen besides the palace in Teleah. Both floors boasted large open archways and windows. Through the largest arched doorway, flanked by elaborate marble columns which resembled trees, Quinn could see a verdant courtyard with a stone fountain.

The entire perimeter of the Villa consisted of rich, vibrant gardens with multiple species of trees, fern, and flowers. A grey stone aqueduct ran toward the west side of the building; Quinn presumed this fed water into the baths and kitchens. To the east, the gardens sloped downward; he could hear a rushing river just out of sight. On the southeastern corner of the Villa, an open-air veranda boasted a massive wooden dining table. An open walkway with ceilings made of wood and vines led from the veranda to the edge of the hill. The air was perfumed with flowers and herbs and a rich smell of soil.

A plump woman in a loose, floral dress approached him from the main entryway, followed by two young men. She wore an apron stained with soot and soil. Her black hair was streaked with grey, and lines framed her blue eyes. She reminded him for just a moment of his mother.

"Quinn." She smiled warmly and took his hand in hers. "Welcome home. I'm Madge, the head of house. Come, I will take you to the library to meet the Sage. These two"—she gestured at the young men behind her— "will take your belongings to your room." Quinn followed her through the garden, politely answering her questions about his journey while trying to take in every aspect of this experience.

Through the main archway, the villa opened into a vast, open corridor that overlooked the green courtyard. The heat of a massive outdoor fireplace warmed the inside of the villa. Opposite the court-yard, the corridor was lined with doors leading to various rooms; he tried to pay attention to everything Madge pointed out.

Madge pushed open a heavy wooden door in the northwest corner of the Villa, revealing the Sage's library. He gasped; he could hardly believe a collection this large existed outside of the Academy. The library was two stories, lined wall to wall with books. A large leather sofa and armchair rested in the middle of the floor. He hoped he would have access to all these books during his apprenticeship.

"Have a seat." Madge pointed at the sofa. "She'll be here in a moment. I'll fetch you in a bit to take you to your room." She left Quinn alone. His wonder and awe subsided into a choking feeling of anxiousness. In any moment, he would meet the most powerful, intelli-gent woman in the world. And somehow, he still found it impossible to believe, he would be her apprentice.

He perched on the edge of the couch, his leg shaking with nerves. Each tick of the clock seemed to take an eternity. He waited for less than five minutes, but he might as well have waited a year. Thoughts of insecurity and doubt crept into his mind. I don't deserve to be here, he told himself. And she'll know it the second I speak.

The door to the library opened, and Quinn stood to greet the Sage. When he saw her, his breath left him. He struggled to keep his mouth from dropping. At least some of the rumors were true.

The Sage of Elandria was not tall, but her presence was simultane-ously unassuming and overwhelming. Her thick brown hair, streaked with sunlight, fell disheveled over her bare shoulders. She wore a purple velvet dress with a plunging neckline and fitted bodice that accentuated her curvy figure. Small, grey eyes seemed to gaze right into his soul as she studied him. Her smile was genuine and warm. If she were anyone else, she would be pretty. But the unostentatious power that emanated from her made her, without a doubt, the most beautiful woman Quinn had ever seen. She crossed the room to greet him.

"My lady Sage," Quinn bowed his head and brought his right hand to his brow, the appropriate greeting for those in positions of power.

She laughed; it was a symphony. "Please, call me Amarice. I hate the formalities when I'm at home." She extended her hand to shake his.

Quinn was taken aback. She seemed so normal. He took her hand, soft to the touch, and breathed in a slight scent of roses. "Amarice," he murmured. "It's an honor." She gave him a wide smile and pulled away, positioning herself on the armchair. She gestured for Quinn to sit on the couch. He sat; she studied him intently, biting her lip and furrowing her brow.

After a few moments, she spoke. "Your professors speak highly of you; they have written to me about you since your first year." Quinn's eyes widened in surprise. "They were correct. Your Gift is immense, but suppressed. Stop wondering if you should be here."

Apparently, she had indeed read his soul with her intense gaze. He dropped his eyes to his lap, trying to process this information. What on earth could his professors have had to say about him to the Sage for the last four years? If his Gift was so strong, why could he not control it? How could she know they were right—could she sense the Gift in others just from meeting them?

"Quinn." He looked up; his name sounded like music on her lips. He pushed down that emotion and tried to focus. "Your very presence emanates wild, unharnessed magic that has been stoppered. You're like a... a... steaming kettle that is intent on exploding boiling water all over the kitchen, but for some reason the lid won't come off." She cocked her head. "I'm sorry. I'm terrible at poetic analogies." She giggled like a schoolgirl, which should have been out-of-character for the Sage of Elandria, but somehow was not. Quinn's thoughts swirled, an inappropriate attraction mingled with confusion and shock at this assessment of his abilities. "Now, tell me what you want to learn. What is it you want to do with your life?"

Quinn forced himself to gather his thoughts. Unfortunately, he did not know what he wanted to do with his life. He always assumed his lack of earth magic would have him teaching in some distant village. For the first time in his life, he let himself imagine all his options. Something about Amarice made nothing in the world seem impossible. "If—if I could do absolutely anything..." He paused and looked at exquisite face. She smiled gently, coaxing him to continue. "I think I would enjoy a career as a minister or a diplomat."

"Oh. Well, I'm definitely not the right person to teach you that." Her voice was deadpan; Quinn stared at her, confused. One of her main roles included advising the royal family and the parliament. Unable to hold the joke, a grin illuminated her visage. Quinn laughed nervously; tales of power and beauty had failed to mention her sarcasm and sense of humor. She spoke again. "Very well. Professor Quickthorn suggested you would make an excellent diplomat. But first we must figure out how to harness that power in you. Now, if you will excuse me, I have a, ahem, meeting to get back to. I'll have Madge show you to your quarters. Dinner is at six; we will speak more then." Amarice rose, and Quinn stood, too, out of respect. She shook his hand once more and turned to leave the library. "Oh, and every apprentice wants to know—yes, you have full access to the library."

Quinn watched the Sage leave, focusing far too much on the swaying of her hips. She was incredible in every way he had not expected. In his mind, Quinn had built her up to be the stuff of legends. He had not anticipated her to be so human. Still, she astounded him.

Madge returned shortly and escorted Quinn to his room off the west corridor. The room was private; Quinn had not had his own room since he was eight years old, when his younger brother was born. He went from sharing the bedroom in his small three-room farmhouse to sharing the dormitory at the Academy with Rafe. He smiled; he would enjoy the alone time. His window overlooked the west garden and the pale green mountains dotted with golds and reds in the distance; he would have an amazing view of the sunset.

His trunk had already been placed in his room. He began to unpack his belongings, neatly folding his clothes in the wardrobe and placing his books on the shelf above the small desk. He placed Rafe's journal on his nightstand. He would have to write his first impressions later. For now, he decided to rest before exploring the grounds. He stretched out on the single bed. He closed his eyes and pictured the Sage. He thought of her face and that purple dress as he fell into dreams.

❦

AMARICE MUSED on her first impressions of her new apprentice. He was handsome, with his neatly parted brown hair and boyish face. He emanated a strong power, stifled by shyness and a lack of confidence. What made him so guarded? She wondered. But there was something else about him that she simply could not place. She wrote it off as simple attraction and climbed the stairs to the room where her latest lover lay waiting.

CHAPTER 6

Quinn entered the veranda a few minutes before six o'clock. The massive oak table seated around twenty people; the head of house and workers sat mingled with Scholars. A spread of fine winter foods lay in wait. Quinn's mouth watered at the smell of roast lamb and the heaping pile of cheesy squash that sat next to it. Madge pointed him to the seat just to the left of the head of the table. He took a seat and waited as few more people drifted into dinner.

A pretty redhead named Daisy sat diagonally across from him. She was an apothecary Scholar who made her full-time residence at the Villa because of the selections of exotic plants Amarice housed in her gardens. She sold her creations to traveling merchants rather than keeping her own shop. She had met Amarice two years ago, and they became fast friends. Quinn chatted with her, reserved but polite, uncomfortable with the flirtatious looks she gave him.

The Sage entered the veranda. She had changed into a royal blue, silk dress and jewel-encrusted silver belt. Her Scholar's pendant drew Quinn's eyes to her breasts. She had braided her hair, accentuating her perfect facial features and deep grey eyes.

Quinn stood out of respect for her position. The moment quickly became awkward. He noticed no one else stood; in fact, no one even seemed to care that the most powerful woman in Elandria had entered the room as they dipped food onto their plates. He sat and felt his face flush with embarrassment. Amarice flashed him a reassuring smile.

Amarice sat at the head of the table next to Quinn. He breathed in her floral scent again. She poured herself a glass of wine and casually expressed her excitement at the bowl of mashed potatoes. "I've been waiting for more potatoes. I had to do magic to protect them from the cold because I could not wait until spring to plant more," she explained to Quinn as she served herself two large heaps of the creamy dish. "Pass the lamb?"

He passed her the platter of meat. "The food is delicious," he said. He saw Madge beam at him from halfway down the table. He helped himself to more squash. Food at the Academy was often stale and bland. He enjoyed the herbaceous flavor of the tender lamb, the earth- iness of the fresh winter vegetables. He hoped every meal would be this satisfying.

"Madge is the best cook in Elandria, I truly believe," Amarice confirmed. "I always worry she will leave me and start a famous restau- rant in the capital." Madge laughed. "So, I just keep paying her well. The Villa couldn't run without her. I'm quite lucky." Amarice spent much of dinner introducing the various residents. She made no distinc- tion between the Scholars and the Villa staff. "Everyone is home for the Feast of Fire," she told Quinn. "It's rare that we are all together without guests. It's just the family tonight."

It did feel like a normal family dinner. In fact, it felt much more like a family than the meals Quinn used to share with his parents and brother. People chatted about their work, about letters they received from family and friends, about the latest news from the capital. Quinn talked to the man to his left; a blond Scholar named Matthew who had been a fourth-year student in Amarice's first-year. He worked as a historian, but he preferred the peace and natural beauty of the Sage's Villa to the drafty Academy offices and busy city.

"Where are you from?" Amarice inquired of Quinn.

He swallowed a bite of Madge's sourdough rolls. "Corthy, in the northern farmlands. About a day's ride from Chyry Vale." Chyry Vale was the only city Quinn had seen before he left his home. After seeing Teleah, he doubted it qualified as a city.

The Sage nodded. "I've visited Chyry Vale. I stay a few days and meet with the northern council on my journeys to the Great Northern Forest. You were near the Lazori border. Did you ever visit Lazoria?"

Quinn shook his head. "No, we rarely left the village. My father owns a farm; there was not much time to get away. The furthest I ever ventured before coming to Teleah was Chyry Vale, and we only went there a handful of times." Quinn had often dreamed of running away to explore Lazoria or the Great Northern Forest. He would study maps of places even further away, but he did not even allow himself to dream of visiting some of those destinations. He knew it would be impossible.

Amarice sensed a feeling of disdain when Quinn mentioned his village. She understood. "I am from Davia, on the peninsula. I never ventured further than a two-day ride from my home before I went to the Academy."

Quinn met her eyes, which were filled with empathy. He had never given much thought to who this woman was before she became the Sage. But in that instance, he saw her as Amarice, a powerful Scholar who had, like him, come from a small village where she likely had her own share of troubles. He wanted to know everything about her. For the first time since receiving the letter from his professor, he felt he might, in fact, be in the right place. He smiled. "I would love to visit the sea," was all he could say.

Dinner progressed with more conversations. When the plates were empty, and no one reached for seconds, Madge and some others began to gather the dishes. Quinn noticed even a couple of the Scholars helped in cleaning up the table. Amarice stacked a few plates and corked the bottle of wine before following the rest of the residents out of the veranda. She gestured to Quinn to follow her. "We often retire to the salon after dinner. We have parlor games and a piano, or sometimes we will just chat."

The salon on the eastern side of the Villa opened directly into the courtyard. A large fireplace glowed next to the windows on the back wall. The walls were lined with brightly colored tapestries and shelves of various artifacts from all over the world. There were tables for parlor games and plush sofas for lounging. A large black piano stood in the corner. A door on the northern wall opened into the Sage's study.

Amarice claimed a chaise lounge for herself, stretching out her legs. Quinn found it hard to believe a woman of such immense power could be so unassuming. She engaged one of the staff members, a game-keeper, in conversation, asking about his mother's health. She knew the lives of every person here, and she genuinely cared. Her mind was far from politics and earth magic. Perhaps that was her real magic: she treated everyone as her equal.

Quinn relaxed on a couch nearby, positioning himself with a clear view of her. He could not deny his attraction to her, although he knew it was inappropriate as her apprentice. But, he figured, just looking would not hurt. He just had to keep himself from staring. Amarice asked him news of the Academy, looking for the latest gossip. She laughed her symphonic laugh at Quinn's stories of professors and shared a few of her own. Her impression of Professor Viridion made Quinn laugh until his gut hurt. Quinn had always been shy and never skilled at small talk, but talking to Amarice was comfortable. He could not remember the last time he felt so at ease.

After several hours, the company had grown smaller. Amarice yawned and stood. She wished Quinn and the remaining people a good night and disappeared through the door to her study. Quinn enjoyed watching her leave. Daisy turned her attention to Quinn and all his normal reservations and anxiety returned. He suddenly wondered if Amarice had used her magic to relax the environment. He knew powerful Scholars could often manipulate the mood of a room, but there was usually an indescribably magical buzz in the air. Quinn had heard nothing. Or maybe she just had a calming presence.

He excused himself from Daisy's company, citing exhaustion from his travels. And he was tired. He peered into the baths, and upon discovering them empty, relaxed in the warm waters perfumed with lavender. No rose, he noticed. He thought of Amarice's scent and replayed her laugh in his mind. She truly was an incredible woman.

IN THE MIDDLE of the night, Quinn woke, drenched in sweat. He sat upright, touching his legs and arms to make sure he was still whole. He searched the dark room for the time: just after three o'clock in the morning. His bedclothes felt confining, and he untangled himself and rose from the bed.

He replayed the dream in his mind. He had dreamed of fire; no, he had dreamed he was on fire. He could feel the burning and hear the screams of others. He saw only flame, and he swore he had smelled burning wood. In fact, he had the feeling in his dream he had been a tree. But trees weren't sentient, and Quinn was very much unburned. He shook himself and opened the door to his bedroom. He needed fresh air.

Quinn looked across the courtyard, surprised to find someone else already there. Illuminated by the moonlight, a woman in a thin white gown knelt on the grass beside the fountain. Her hands were in the water. Though he had met her only twelve hours prior, he recognized her instantly.

He walked out of the corridor through the stone arches into the courtyard. The wet grass under his feet felt refreshingly cold after his dream of burning. As he drew nearer to Amarice, he heard her weeping. He stood for a moment, unsure whether to leave her or approach. Finally, he spoke. "Amarice?" She turned, surprised to see him standing there. She pulled her hands from the fountain and wiped her eyes.

"Did you dream?" she asked, a sob catching on her throat. Quinn nodded and told her what he had dreamed. "I dreamt the same," she whispered. "I felt I was on fire, so I came to touch the water." She did not speak for a few minutes. Quinn wondered what it all meant; what was this nightmare he shared with the Sage? Amarice cut across his thoughts. "Professor Quickthorn told me of your first dream the night those Scholars were murdered. I had the same dream. As far as I have learned, no one else but you shared this."

"Why?" Quinn murmured, his voice barely audible. "Why us?"

Amarice shrugged her shoulders. "I wish I knew. Have you dreamt any others?"

"No...yes." He recalled the dream he had the night he went out with Jack and Rafe. He told her of the music and colors that had been swallowed by the darkness, and how he assumed it had been an alcohol-infused dream.

"And the blast of a horn?" He nodded. She had dreamed the same dream. "That night, twenty Deyoni were slaughtered with no warning and no way to defend themselves. The king's Inquisitors have no leads. And unfortunately, few people seem to care because they were Deyoni." She sighed. "I fear what this latest dream means."

CHAPTER 7

Quinn did not see Amarice much the following day. She had sequestered herself away in her study, shutting all the doors that opened to the courtyard. At breakfast, she was cheery, but she did not speak much.

Quinn spent most of the day exploring the grounds of the Villa. He went for a run along the river, enjoying the fresh mountain air. He relished in the quiet; for once there were no distant voices distracting him when he tried to be alone. He heard only the sound of birds and the wind, the braying of sheep down the southern slope of the mountain.

He wandered through the verdant gardens, studying the plants. Someone, he assumed the Sage, had meticulously marked all the plants with stone markers, even those that were in hibernation until spring. He knew many of the plants, but others he had only read about in his textbooks. Jack would be ecstatic, Quinn thought. In the northern garden, he followed a stone path that led to a clearing with a lone tree. He ventured closer to determine the species.

But it was not one tree; it was two. An oak and a pine had grown together. Their trunks curved, intertwined. They stood together, still two separate trees, but inextricably linked. Quinn studied the trees with interest. He had never seen such a phenomenon. Typically, if trees grew too close together, the stronger would take root and the other would fail to thrive. Not these. He ran his hand over the bark of each. These trees were old; he could feel their ancient connection to the earth.

"It's called the Consort's Tree," a melodic voice startled him. He turned to find Amarice standing near him. Her flowing green dress flapped in the breeze. Her hair was loose again and blew wildly around her face. She stepped closer to the tree and Quinn, reaching out to touch the trunks. "The story goes that when the Sage Gwen finally took her lover to her bed, these trees grew overnight from nothing. No one had planted seeds or saplings here. No other trees grow in this clearing. They discovered it the next day. Gwen, as I'm sure you know, became the first Sage to name a Consort."

"That's impossible," Quinn said. "Trees can't grow from nothing. And the Sage's bed is too far for earth magic to have any effect."

Amarice smiled. "Indeed. It does seem the stuff of folk tales. Nothing of the sort has happened since, despite several Sages naming Consorts."

Quinn recalled what he had learned from his history classes. Sage's Consorts were rare; many Sages had long-time lovers and occasionally even spouses before marriage went out of style. But a Consort required an incredibly deep level of trust. They must be Scholars, and they must know the Sage well enough to act on her behalf. If the Sage names a Consort, he or she becomes the second-most powerful political and social force outside of the Royal Family, after the Sage. Indeed, many historians argue the Sage is in fact a more powerful force than the king or Queen. But the strength of the Gift of the reigning Sage coupled with the immense responsibility that comes with the role is isolating. Few Sages ever grew to trust someone so completely that they would be named Consort. When they did, the Consorts went on to become great leaders and voices in the history of Elandria.

Amarice smiled her lovely smile and walked away to the river without saying a word. He saw her again, briefly, at dinner, but she did not go to the salon to socialize. Quinn did not feel like making small talk with anyone, either. He bathed quickly and retired to his room for the evening. He sat at his small desk and wrote in the journal Rafe had given him. Perhaps one day a book about apprenticing with the Sage would sell, he considered. He wrote down all he could remember from the last day and a half. He composed letters to Rafe and Jack, although he left out too much description of the Sage's beauty; he did not want them to know they were right.

That night, Quinn slept dreamlessly. The next day would bring the Feast of Fire, and then his apprenticeship would officially begin.

⚜

THE MORNING BROKE clear and bright. Quinn made his way to the veranda for breakfast, eager to see what the day's celebrations would bring. The Feast of Fire traditionally did not start until sundown, and it had always been Quinn's favorite holiday.

He took his seat and greeted the table happily. Amarice sipped her coffee at the head of the table, chatting with Daisy about a friend from the capital. Quinn served himself some bread and cheese and listened to their conversation. Apparently, their friend had traveled abroad on a diplomatic trip and returned home with a husband from a distant country. "I just don't understand why she would get married," Daisy shook her head.

"Well, marriage is expected in her culture." Amarice poured herself more coffee. "Still, he must be something special if she's willing to give her life to just one man. I can't imagine." She looked at Quinn. "What do you think, Quinn? About marriage?"

He swallowed of bite of his breakfast. "I nearly got married once." Daisy's eyes widened; Amarice appraised him. "It... didn't work out. But if she's the right one, I understand." He took another bite of bread and chewed thoughtfully.

"How on earth are you supposed to know if someone is the right one?" Daisy asked, intrigued. Amarice stayed quiet, still staring at Quinn. This young man had some shadows in his past; she wondered what he failed to say.

"I don't know." He smiled wistfully. "I haven't figured that part out."

Amarice changed the subject, and Quinn felt thankful. He had not intended to share that; even Rafe never knew Quinn had planned to marry Elaine, nor what had transpired his last day in Corthy. He lost himself in his own thoughts for a bit.

Quinn studied Amarice as Daisy droned on about nothing. He wondered if her village had been as anti-magic as his. He wanted to ask her, to know every detail of her life. He wanted to tell her everything about his life, every thought he had. Unsure from whence this desire came, he suppressed the urge and pushed his feelings down further.

After breakfast, Quinn went for a run on the grounds again. Nothing cleared his thoughts like his feet pounding the earth, the crisp air filling his lungs. He once again found himself at the Consort's Tree. He doubted the legend was true, but he was intrigued by the adaptability of the two trees. More leaves had fallen since yesterday in the winter wind. He reached out to a nearly-barren branch. He could not remember the last time he had tried to channel his Gift. He focused all his energy on growing a leaf, just one leaf.

He could not. Revitalizing a dying plant by touch was considered basic earth magic. He could feel the magic fill him, but he could not manipulate it to his will. "Damn it!" He banged a fist against the trunk of the tree.

He gasped. Both trees had fully bloomed, bright green leaves contrasting with the warm colors of autumn surrounding him. In his anger with himself, he had made the tree look as if winter had never touched its branches. He felt a mix of both amazement and frustration. His magic only worked in fits of anger, and even then, he could not do what he intended. He studied the branches for a moment longer then turned to go back to the Villa.

Amarice stood at the edge of the garden, watching. He met her eyes. She smiled, a look of understanding on her face. Then she turned and walked away.

QUINN ENTERED the courtyard a few hours later to find everyone preparing for the night's celebrations. The dining table had been moved near the fountain, and several people constructed a pile of wood for the bonfire. Large vases of soil had been moved into the courtyard; Amarice moved among them, waving a hand over the soil. Green strands of magic energy flowed from her fingers, blooming chrysanthemums of vibrant red and gold. Chrysanthemums were important to the Feast of Fire; not only did they look like vases of fire, they represented grief and lamentation. At the end of the night, every person would name their grief and throw a flower into the flames.

He helped Matthew and some of the others construct the bonfire. Though the Feast of Fire was a holiday of death and grief, everyone was cheerful. The holiday was cleansing, drawing the year to a close and helping to release each person of their burdens. Tomorrow, a new year would begin. Quinn loved the introspection and symbolism that came with the Feast of Fire. Today, especially, felt significant. Not only would a new year begin tomorrow, but a new chapter of his life as his apprenticeship with the Sage commenced.

The appearance of a young man no one knew caused everyone to stop their tasks and stare, confused. He wore the blue tunic of the Messengers. Even Messengers did not work on the Feast of Fire, yet this young man looked harried and held an envelope in his hand. Something must be wrong. Amarice approached him, a look of concern on her face.

"My lady Sage." The Messenger drew his hand to his brow in greeting. "An urgent message." The young man looked as if he would collapse any moment.

"Are you well?" Amarice took the envelope but did not open it. Her concern for the Messenger outweighed her concern for the message.

"With the holiday, I rode my horse twice the normal distance. There were few Messengers to be found along the road. We're exhausted, my Lady."

"You must rest. I'll have my gamekeeper see to your horse, and my head-of-house will take you to a room to sleep. You can spend the Feast of Fire with us." He bowed his head in thanks. The gamekeeper and Madge hurried forward and escorted him out of the courtyard.

Amarice studied the envelope for several moments before opening it. The residents of the Villa watched her silently, barely daring to breathe. Quinn saw her hand shake slightly as she opened the letter. Her face turned stony as she read. She turned slowly and began to walk in the direction of her study. "Quinn," she said. Quinn met Matthew's eyes in surprise; Matthew shrugged. Unsure why Amarice wanted to see him, and only him, Quinn followed her to her study.

"Shut the door." She sat behind her large rosewood desk. Quinn obliged, not sure what to do next. She held out the letter for him to read. "Our dream." She pressed her hands against her eyes.

Quinn took the letter. He read it three times, hoping he would understand. The Forest of Seluya had been burned. An estimated quarter of the third-largest forest in Elandria was gone before enough Scholars gathered to control the flames. Burning a forest was one of the highest crimes in Elandria. Indeed, for every tree that is even chopped down for building or firewood, a new sapling must be planted. A quarter of the forest! Quinn could not fathom it. Judging by the Sage's reaction, Amarice could not fathom it either. His heart ached for the loss of the trees.

"Did we... foresee this?"

Amarice shook her head. "No, it seems every dream we have had happened while the attacks were occurring." She leaned back in her chair, eyes closed.

"But why?"

"I have a theory, but I have no proof." Quinn waited for her to continue. "These attacks are on earth magic itself. Our Gift is so much stronger, so we can feel it happening." She laughed dryly, no humor to be heard. "I hope you have no more doubts that you are quite power-ful, Quinn. For better or worse."

Quinn sank onto an armchair and examined the room. Her walls were lined with books and brightly colored tapestries, contrasting with the darkness he felt. No fire burned in the fireplace; she had not antici-pated working today. He shivered, making the Sage aware of the cold. She held a hand toward the fireplace; a small flame grew from the logs inside. Amazing, he thought. Even the more powerful Scholars he had met had to be within a foot of the fire and there had to be embers to grow a flame. He wondered what else she could do that no one else could.

He looked at her, her eyes darkened with grief. Despite her obvious grief, she was still beautiful. She clutched the Scholar's pendant at her breast, as if for guidance. Quinn broke the silence. "What do we do?"

She opened her deep, grey eyes and met his brown ones. "Tonight is the Feast of Fire. We grieve." She stood. "Tell the others what happened. We will continue the holiday as planned." She crossed the study and disappeared through the door that led to her private rooms.

◈❧◈

CANDLES ILLUMINATED the piles of food on the table as Quinn entered the courtyard. The sky shifted from blue to shades of orange and pink as the sun prepared to sleep for the night. The aroma of smoked meats mingled with the scent of rich spices. Carafes of crimson fire-wine lined the table; Quinn longed for a drink to warm himself in the wintry evening.

He ran a hand through his hair to make sure it lay in place. He had opted for his finest attire in honor of his first holiday at the Villa: leather pants and tunic the color of midnight over a red silk shirt. As he had dressed with care, he had tried to tell himself his motives were solely the holiday. Truthfully, he had imagined Amarice as he combed his hair and laced his tunic.

No one sat at the table yet; instead the Villa residents stood in small groups, whispering. The mood at the Villa had shifted significantly when Quinn re-entered the courtyard and told them the news of Seluya. They had finished the preparations in silence. Now, hours later, Quinn noticed the young Messenger standing alone in the corner of the courtyard; he looked more rested but nervous. Quinn approached him and greeted him kindly. He, too, still felt out of place. Amarice had not arrived to grace the holiday with her calming presence; in fact, no one had seen her since she disappeared into her private quarters that afternoon.

The Messenger, Brian, told Quinn how he and a colleague had sat in their post, waiting for sunrise when they could go home for the holiday. Another Messenger approached, his horse stumbling from the strain of the ride. "One to the king and one to the Sage," he had told

Brian and the other Messenger. "Don't stop until it's in their hands." Brian and his horse rode 100 miles without rest to get to the Sage's Villa. Quinn could sense his concern for his horse and assured Brian the gamekeeper would take good care of her.

The sun set further. With the last hint of light in the sky, Amarice entered from her study. Quinn and the Messenger both gasped. For the first time since his arrival, Quinn saw her as the immensely powerful legend he had always imagined. Although, he never imagined the degree of her beauty.

Her full skirt, which had been dyed the colors of fire, swirled red, orange, yellow as she moved. Above her bare midriff, her top jingled with coins and shells. She had painted her lips a deep red and decorated her face with jewels that shimmered in the low light. She had pinned her luscious brown hair on the top of her head and tucked a red flower behind her left ear. She carried a burning torch and approached the bonfire.

Drums played as she walked. Quinn looked for the source of the music; the gamekeeper and a farmhand were dressed in full Deyoni garb—wide pants in vibrant colors paired with velvety vests on their bare chests. Two of the maids approached the fire, dressed in the same fashion as the Sage, hips swaying to the slow rhythm of the drums. Amarice's voice rung clear across the courtyard: *"Adawe draba mulo galisa—oyua atsila!"* She flung the torch onto the wood; the drums beat faster. She raised her hands from the earth to sky, and the fire spread over the whole pile instantly.

She turned and began to dance. The other two followed her in perfect time. Quinn could not peel his eyes away. These were not the folk dances with which he was familiar. Her hips bounced and swirled, quicker than the drumbeat. When she turned, her skirts swirled as if she were the fire. The beats slowed; she slowed. Her body waved with the ease of the ocean tide. When she slowed, the fire slowed; when she danced faster, so did the fire.

Quinn felt overcome with emotion, but for once, he felt safe in it. As he watched, darkness poured from him and fire entered him, not to harm, but to cleanse. His feet seemed to grow into the earth; he felt the earth's magic flow through him and unite with the magic that emanated from the Sage's dancing and into the surrounding air. The wind blew loudly, so the drums grew louder. The bonfire crackled, the fountain spit, and the earth vibrated. The elements made their own music, and the Sage matched their rhythm with her hips.

The dancing and the drums stopped. The earth stopped moving. Amarice gathered an armful of chrysanthemums from a nearby vase. She spoke the names of the two slaughtered Scholars and tossed two flowers to burn. "The innocent Deyoni," she said. Twenty flowers flew into the flames. A few more went into the fire without a word. She held one last flower in her hand and gazed at it a long time. "The Forest of Seluya." She tossed the last flower into the bonfire, gazing as it incinerated. She turned away, and one by one, the others brought their flowers and named their griefs. Some spoke audibly the names of loved ones lost; some only whispered, because only the fire needed to hear their grief.

Quinn took one flower and drew forward. The flames were scalding. "To my old life," he whispered so only the fire would hear. And he tossed the red chrysanthemum into the blaze.

The feast began. Quinn felt a lightness he had not felt in a long time. People chatted happily, glad to unburden themselves from the year's grief. Even Amarice seemed happier. "Tonight, we grieve. Tomorrow, we find solutions," she told him. He asked her about the dance. "The dance of mulo. My mother was Deyoni. The Feast of Fire was their holiday first."

"It was unlike anything I have ever seen."

"You've never seen Deyoni dance magic?" She seemed surprised. The Deyoni often danced for money around Elandria.

He shook his head. "I was never allowed to go see them. Is it earth magic, though?"

"In its purest form." She poured herself a glass of fire-wine. Quinn had never learned that the Deyoni were magic at the Academy. His parents had always said they were demon-worshippers, but he wrote that off as superstition. He made a note to ask Amarice more and to write about it to Rafe.

Daisy began the tradition of naming the year's favorite memories. People laughed at everyone's stories. Though the night was about grieving losses, it was also about the death of a year. Quinn reflected on his year as he listened. What was his favorite memory? He thought of nights out with his friends, of great classes and good marks. To his right, Amarice rattled off a story of a journey to the sea she had made in the summer. As he listened to her melodic voice, he knew.

"Quinn, your turn." Amarice touched his hand. He swore he felt a jolt of lightning rush through him at her touch. He smiled.

"When I received word of my apprenticeship." He took a drink of fire-wine; the smoky liquid mingled with a touch of cinnamon burned his throat. He nodded at Matthew to his left to tell his story. Quinn turned his head to look at Amarice, her grey eyes dancing in the fire-light. She gazed into his soul and smiled. He wished she would touch him again.

The night continued with toasts and laughter. Slowly, people went off to their rooms. The Feast of Fire was supposed to end with private reflection; though the wine and intimacy of the night had many pairing off, arms intertwined. Quinn watched Amarice approach the fire and bring the flames down to a controllable level. She disappeared not into her chambers, but into the western wing with a beautiful Scholar on her arm. Quinn fought a twinge of jealousy and disappeared into his room, alone.

CHAPTER 8

Quinn glanced at the clock and sighed. He had taken up residence in the library for the last three hours, reading a dry tome about the art of diplomacy. He marked his page and closed the book; he could not take much more of the tedious writing of some Scholar from three hundred years ago. He wondered where Amarice was. She had told him they would take a walk on the grounds later.

It was the third day of his apprenticeship, but Quinn could not help but feel like he was on an extended vacation. Her tasks for him included getting to know the Villa residents and taking advantage of a library without waiting lists. She had said she wanted him to "ease into" his apprenticeship, whatever that meant. He had spent the morning asking a few of the Scholars about their diplomatic work, then settled himself into the library's leather sofa with a stack of books.

He considered going for a run or seeing if the baths were unoccupied. Or perhaps he could nap: that damn book had bored him to the point of exhaustion. He stared into space, weighing his options when the Sage entered.

Although he had been at the Villa for a week, she still took Quinn's breath away whenever she entered a room. He wondered if he would ever grow complacent to her beauty and hoped he would not. Today, she had braided her hair, and it rested over her shoulder. Her open-backed, sapphire dress fit snugly over her arms and bosom before flowing like water over her hips. She carried a sense of peace with her into every room she entered.

"You have a letter," she told him and placed an envelope in his hand. He turned it over. Rafe. He missed his best friend already. Quinn thanked her and opened the envelope, surprised to find a five-page letter inside.

He could hear his friend's voice through his letter. He gave every detail of the Academy's Feast of Fire celebration—and the after-party. Jack had reached the point of drunkenness that he broke down in tears, wailing about selecting the right apprenticeship and career path. Rafe assured him it had been quite pathetic, and Jack enjoyed his first day with the old apothecary immensely. "Sarah has become quite the bitch," he wrote. "I think she misses you." Quinn doubted it; he was sure anger motivated her instead. He gave him the details of Professor Viridion's magic cohort. "I manipulated the air around me today into a soundproof bubble and grew embers into flame from nearly two feet away. I'm excited to continue pushing the limits of my Gift." He also wrote about the mass burning in the Forest of Seluya. The Scholars in the region are overwhelmed and are having trouble planting saplings in the scorched earth, he wrote. Messengers have been pouring into the Academy excessively.

He looked up when he finished reading. Amarice had a stack of letters of her own. She read them quickly, penning a short reply to each. She used the book Quinn had been reading earlier as a makeshift desk.

Amarice caught Quinn staring and smiled. She held up the book guiltily. "It's about all this damn thing is good for," she said dryly. He laughed in agreement. "Who was your letter from?"

"My roommate from school, Rafe." Once again, he found himself sharing more details of his life with her, describing his friendship with

Rafe from their first day at the Academy. She listened intently, laughing at his funny stories about his friend.

"He sounds quite special."

"He sure thinks he is," Quinn replied, an unmistakable tone of affection in his voice. Though still immensely private, Quinn had shared more about himself with Amarice in the last few days than he had shared with anyone. Minutia, mostly, but Amarice could read much of the emotion that lay behind his stories. He changed the subject. "Do you have any news from the capital?"

She shook her head. "Only that the king has dispatched extra Inquisitors to investigate. Most of my mail has been from Scholars wondering how to grow trees in dead earth."

"Is it possible?"

Amarice's smile illuminated her face; her eyes wild with excitement. "Meet me at the Consort's Tree in just a few minutes." She bounced away. Her habit of leaving without explanation or farewell added to her mystery. He laughed to himself and wondered what she wanted to show him.

⁂

TEN MINUTES LATER, Quinn met the Sage at the Consort's Tree. She now wore a velvet cloak in deep crimson over her dress. It was cold today, but he had not seen her wear anything of the sort before. The red suited her well. "I need all my magic for what I'm about to show you. I won't be able to keep myself warm," she explained. "Come."

He followed her through the clearing and down the slope of the mountain. She stopped at a random point and sat on the grass. He crossed his legs and sat next to her. "The problem," she told him, "is that the Scholars in Seluya are trying to channel the earth's life into the saplings rather than the earth itself." She pulled a box of matches from her cloak and lit one. "Forgive me," she whispered, not to Quinn but to the earth itself as if it were sentient. She set the flame to the grass, and, using her magic to create a small boundary for the fire, watched as the flame grew and singed the earth. "Tell me, Quinn, what you know of the Law of Connection."

Quinn knew the laws of earth magic well; it was only the execution with which he struggled. "The Gift can only be harnessed by connection to the element. If you cannot physically touch what you wish to manipulate, you must be near enough to envision a cord connecting you." The Sage nodded in approval. She did not speak again until the flames died to a slow spark. He tried to memorize the curves of her face as she watched the fire.

Finally, she broke the silence. "The Scholars in Seluya are trying to pull life from the burned topsoil or from other plants to grow new saplings. But nothing can grow in dead soil. Instead they must connect to the earth that still lives, deep below the topsoil, and pull the life from there."

"But... you cannot see down that far. How can the Law of Connection apply?"

She smiled. "What they fail to teach you at the Academy is the Law of Connection is not a law, but a tool. You are the connection; that is why you are a Scholar. We are inherently connected to the heart of the earth. I've caused quite the controversy with the idea. It's just not tangible enough for most Scholars to want to accept."

Quinn understood the unwillingness of Scholars to accept the Sage's idea. He needed tangible and rational in his life. But perhaps, he mused, not everything is so neatly explained. He ran his fingers through the grey soil, crumbled and dead beneath his hands.

Amarice placed both her palms on the circle of burned earth and inhaled. Her eyes were closed. He watched as she slowed her breathing in concentration. Quinn felt a tingle in the air. Streams of visible magic flowed from her hands into the earth. After a few minutes, he saw the soil change before his eyes. The scorched grey slowly turned into the rich, black soil it had been before. The Sage moved her palms, electric with magic, over the area, revitalizing the earth into a living entity once again. Once the area was refreshed, she opened her eyes. She placed her right hand in the air, and a gust of wind came to wash away the last bit of burned dust. Quinn had no words, only awe.

Amarice removed her cloak and lay on the ground, eyes closed again. She looked weak, and he knew that had taken a considerable amount of her magic. He did not speak as she pulled the Gift of the Earth into her body. He simply admired her as she lay, both for her immense power and knowledge and for her exquisiteness. He fought the urge to touch her face.

After a few minutes, the Sage sat up and spoke. "Normally I would have meditated beforehand so as not to deplete my magic so quickly." She stood, and Quinn followed. As she tried to take a step, she stumbled. Quinn took her arm in his to support her. Amarice smiled and accepted his support, too weak to pull away and walk alone yet. Both she and Quinn suppressed a feeling of how right it seemed to walk with their arms interlaced.

"Will you go to Seluya to help?"

"No. I thought about it, but other Scholars must learn to do the magic themselves. Intuition tells me I should stay here. I'm the leader of the Scholars, not their crutch." Her strength returned with every step she took, the Gift of the Earth flowing from the ground through her bare feet. But she did not pull away from Quinn.

"Amarice, do you know why I cannot control my Gift?"

"Yes."

"Why?" he inquired.

She smiled. "You must figure that out for yourself. You will, soon. I'm sure of it." She finally pulled away as they passed the Consort's Tree. "I will see you at dinner." She turned toward her private chambers and walked away from him. He stared after her, wishing he could have followed her. He wanted to know more—more about earth magic, more about her, more about himself.

He returned to the library with much to ponder. Only in his bursts of anger had he ever seen tangible magic. But small bolts of lightning streamed from the Sage's hands when she performed powerful magic. He knew of no other Scholar who could do this. Her insight on the Law of Connection, and his observation of it, had rocked his entire knowledge of magical laws.

And she knew why he could not harness his earth magic, but she would not tell him. He had spent years trying to figure out why he could not control his Gift. What made her so sure he would figure it out soon? He sighed and collapsed on the oversized armchair in the library. He did not understand.

He mused over these new discoveries in silence until dinner. But he gained no new insight, and he had trouble keeping his thoughts from how it had felt to walk arm-in-arm with Amarice. *Get it together, Quinn,* he told himself.

CHAPTER 9

Two weeks later, Quinn sat in Amarice's study reading yet another book about diplomacy while she answered her letters. He glanced up occasionally to watch her. Her brow furrowed whenever she wrote quickly and intensely. If she needed to stop and think, she ran her hands through her hair. Sometimes she blurted random obscenities and mumbled under her breath. He had enjoyed learning her quirks and habits, and by now, she seemed fully human to him—no longer a mythical power.

Despite his attraction and respect, he had settled into a routine and could not help feeling that he had learned hardly anything. She gave him no structured lessons, no lists of required reading. He still had not figured out why he could not do earth magic, and she still refused to tell him. She kept saying to just "get used to life at the Villa." His frustration had increased tenfold the last few days, though he suppressed his negativity.

Amarice spoke suddenly. "I have been summoned to the palace for a meeting with the king and the Chief Inquisitor. I hope they have some leads. I will be gone a couple days."

"Will I be going?" Quinn asked, a trace of hope leaking into his voice.

"No, not this time. Just stay here and have some fun. Matthew has returned from his trip. I'm sure he has some interesting stories." She went back to writing her letters. Quinn felt a burst of anger growing, and he could not control it.

"Brigitte's tit! I did not come here for a damned extended vacation!" Flames leapt from the fireplace as he yelled. His outbursts of emotion were dangerous. He froze, unsure what to do as the fire spread across the floor.

Amarice waved her hand with an infuriating nonchalance and the flames danced their way back into the fireplace. Her Deyoni-woven rug had burned to a crisp. "I liked that rug," she said with no hint of emotion in her voice.

Quinn bowed his head, embarrassed, and sank into a chair. He felt his face grow hot. "I'm sorry. That was unacceptable. It won't happen again."

The Sage laughed. Quinn looked at her, shocked. He could not figure out what was funny. He had yelled at the most powerful woman in Elandria and nearly set her study on fire. But she sat behind her desk, laughing. He did not know what to say.

"You still don't get it, do you, Quinn? Your magic only manifests, and manifests quite strongly, when you let yourself feel. I've given you this 'extended vacation' as you called it to force you into frustration and to break you of your need to have structure. Your very essence screams your need of structure and rules because you use that to suppress every emotion you have. I do not know what happened in your past that has caused you to stifle every feeling. But the Gift of the Earth is a gift of emotion. You will continue to suppress your earth magic for as long as you suppress the emotions that make you human."

Quinn sat, stunned. No one had ever spoken this way to him. No one had ever read his soul so accurately. And suddenly, everything made sense. The mental block Professor Viridion had described was the block he had placed on himself. But he had spent the last twenty-four years learning to suppress anything he felt. He was unsure how to stop. And he felt scared: scared of the wild magic that came with his outbursts and scared of the hurt in his heart he had never confronted.

His mind flew back to Corthy. He could hear the voices of the village adults whenever he made something happen on accident, speaking of sin and evil. He remembered the fear the other children had of him, the isolation he had from everyone except Elaine and his brother. He remembered trying to earn his father's approval and love but never succeeding. And he remembered his mother's eyes, kind and filled with love, but also with sadness and shame. His very existence had tarnished his family's reputation.

A lump grew in his throat. "They thought I was possessed by demons," he whispered. He could not bear to look at Amarice. If he had, he would have seen her eyes fill with tears, her face flush with empathy.

"Oh, Quinn." She did not push the matter. She simply watched him stew in his memories, fighting the urge to run to his side and offer him comfort. After a long while, he cleared his throat and raised his head to meet her eyes. "Go. You have reflection to do. I will return in two days. We will speak more then."

He murmured a word of thanks and left her study. He did not attend dinner that night nor breakfast the next morning. Her heart ached for him, but she could not help him until he helped himself grow.

❧

AMARICE LEFT the next day after breakfast. She thought of Quinn the entire ride to the palace. His brown eyes had been overwhelmed by sadness. She wondered if she had done the right thing by not offering him comfort. She smiled as she remembered when they had walked together weeks before. But Quinn was her apprentice; in a few months' time, he would be gone. She took a page from his book and suppressed the emotions that had begun to develop and focused her energy on the news the king would have for her.

She met with the king and Chief Inquisitor as soon as she arrived. King Roland, a jolly man with chocolate skin and a large round belly, was one of her favorite people in the world. Her history with Prince

Raymond at the Academy had given her a unique role among the Royal Family. Though Sages were always the closest advisors of the king, Roland was the closest thing she had ever had to a father.

King Roland greeted her cheerfully in his study. The Chief Inquisitor, a stern, older man named Marcus Congreve, stood and gave her the salute of greeting. She assumed her role as Sage instead of Amarice, and listened to the news from the country.

"You were right, my lady Sage," Marcus told her. "We believe the three attacks are related, although we don't know how. However, there have been reports of a growing suspicion of Scholars and Deyoni in the outlying villages. My men have heard rumors of travelers who talk of the evils of earth magic. Most people have written these stories off as some dated religion."

"Do we know who these people are?" the Sage replied in a flat voice.

"No, my lady. Just folks passing through. We are not even sure if they are Elandrians. I have men stationed in villages throughout the country to find out what they can."

The king spoke for the first time. "Amarice, do you think it could be the Lazori? They have been quite frustrated with our terms for the latest trade agreement. I know they believe in evil magic."

Amarice did not know. It could be the Lazori, but she felt villagers would recognize the travelers as foreign. She thought it far more likely to be a political group responding the new laws regarding the Deyoni and the protection of the earth. She knew many in small towns hated the work she and other Scholars had done to increase the rights of the Deyoni. Perhaps the two Scholars who had been slaughtered in their inn were advocates for the nomadic people. But that did not explain why these people, whoever they were, would burn a forest. They discussed their theories some more.

"As always, keep me informed. I will go through the histories to see if I can find anything that sounds similar."

The Chief Inquisitor thanked her and excused himself. "Are you quite all right, Amarice?" King Roland asked her. She shrugged. He appraised her, but he did not push her to talk more. "Very well. Thank you for coming into town. How is your new apprentice doing?"

Amarice grinned, despite herself. "Well," she replied. "His Gift is quite strong." The king studied her face, as if he wanted to ask more, but he did not. He excused himself to a meeting with ministers from the parliament, and Amarice left the study to walk among the palace gardens to meditate.

CHAPTER 10

Amarice's laughter rang through the air like the perfect song. Quinn laughed, too, happiness and pride filling his soul. He had just grown a small harvest of asparagus from seed to stalk for the first time. "We're eating that tonight!" she exclaimed. "Excellent work." She pulled herself up from the ground in the eastern garden and dusted the dirt off the back of her pale blue dress.

A month had passed since Amarice's trip to the palace. Quinn's abilities had undergone a drastic improvement. Though he kept his emotions to himself most of the time, he had practiced opening himself up to harness his Gift. Fire seemed to be the easiest for him to control. The last week he had taken to starting every fireplace in the Villa himself. For fun, he would raise and shrink the flames, while everyone around him shivered. Amarice was unsure what he would do as the weather grew warmer and there was no need for fireplaces.

He still struggled with growing plants, and he spent hours every day with buckets of seeds in the garden. He had no control over water at all, but he had successfully changed the direction of the breeze the day before. Whenever he grew frustrated, jolts of visible magic would shoot from his fingers, but he had worked hard to ensure it caused no danger. He did not want to incinerate any more of the Sage's belongings.

Amarice learned to recognize his frustration before it boiled over. Whenever Quinn struggled with a block on his magic, she instructed him to take an inventory of his emotions. Today, in a fit of asparagus-inspired anger, he had told her he kept imagining the misery of farming with his father. He shook himself; he had never told anyone of the strained father-son relationship he had known his whole life. And yet, telling Amarice just seemed right.

As always, she listened with empathy. She had let him sit in silence for a few minutes before she told him to try again. He placed his hand on the soil over the spot where the seeds lay beneath the ground, and imagined himself pulling the stalks from the earth. What felt like flames left his palm, and he could feel the growth of the seeds beneath the dirt. Slowly, he moved his hand away, and the stalks of asparagus followed the trails of magic. Soon, he had about a dozen stalks of asparagus.

She turned to walk back to the Villa. "That won't feed too many people," she said, a hint of teasing in her voice. "Grow some more." Quinn laughed and watched her walk away, one of his favorite pastimes.

With his newfound abilities, Quinn's confidence had grown, as well. He acted less shy around everyone at the Villa, especially Amarice. They spent hours every day together, often just talking. She imparted her knowledge of politics and diplomacy. He gave her his thoughts and interpretations on history and laws. Often, they would enter the veranda for dinner together, continuing a lighthearted debate on something historical or political, much to the chagrin of most of the Villa's residents, who had grown bored with their overtly Scholar discussions.

His letters to Rafe raved about his life at the Villa. He wrote in detail the things he learned about earth magic, hoping it would be of some use to his friend. He told him what he had learned of the Deyoni: how they, too, had earth magic but not in the same way the Scholars did. He told him the Sage's perspective on the Deyoni's history, that their lands were taken by the earliest settlers in the Valley and were squashed when they rose to defend themselves. "They are an old people, the oldest in Elandria. They are not savage and simple. We should not be so quick to dismiss them. I believe Scholars have much to learn from their ancient magic," Quinn wrote.

No new attacks had occurred, and the king's Inquisitors had no further leads. Amarice was cautiously hopeful that the attacks had ended for good. Still, the Deyoni feared for their safety, and more and more tribes poured into and around Teleah. Scholars in the Forest of Seluya made slow but steady progress in revitalizing the forest as they learned how to do the magic of which Amarice had written.

Many of the Villa's Scholars had left to travel for their work, and occasionally visitors would arrive for a day or two. Sometimes they were friends of the Villa residents; other times Amarice met with members of Parliament who sought her advice on proposed legislation. Quinn learned much from these meetings.

Overall, the mood at the Villa was bright. Quinn now felt completely at home. The days grew longer, and the weather grew warmer. Quinn was the happiest he had ever been.

One afternoon, he heard voices coming from the library as he went to grab a book he wanted. He stopped himself pushing open the door when he heard his name. Ignoring his moral compass telling him not to eavesdrop, he paused and listened to the conversation.

"Amarice, if you would just sleep with him for all of our sakes. Especially yours." Daisy's voice carried through the walls.

"I don't know what you're talking about. He's my apprentice, nothing more."

"That's never stopped you before."

"Drop it, Daisy." Amarice's voice held a warning.

"Amarice, I'm speaking as your friend. I've never seen you like this."

"This conversation is over." The door to the library flung open, and Amarice looked at Quinn with wide eyes.

He stammered an apology, and she pushed past him without a word. Daisy followed, offering a look of sympathy at Quinn as she passed.

Quinn waited until the corridor had cleared before returning to his room. He slammed his fist on his door in frustration. He knew Amarice regularly took lovers, sometimes residents of the Villa, other times visitors from the capital. He had to fight off a monster of jealousy every time someone mentioned sleeping with Amarice.

He lay on his bed. Of course, he wanted her, but his attraction was so much deeper than just physical. He felt drawn to her mind, to her humor. He still felt amazed by her every second they were together. But Quinn was shy and inexperienced; he was also her apprentice. He had forced himself to fight his desire for her except in the deepest hours of the night. He had believed he would never have her because it would be inappropriate.

But now he felt confused. Apparently, Amarice had no problem bedding with her apprentices. Perhaps she wasn't attracted to Quinn, but Daisy made it sound otherwise. Maybe she could sense his innocence and did not want an inexperienced lover. But he wanted to be more than her lover. He was falling in love with the Sage of Elandria, the most powerful woman to ever walk the earth.

He screamed into his pillow.

❦

CHOKING. Gasping. Quinn struggled for air, fighting back against his faceless assailant. He grasped at his neck to no avail. He felt himself grow weaker, darkness filling his thoughts until he could see nothing, feel nothing. He was gone.

Quinn bolted upright from his bad, gasping for air. It took him several minutes to slow his breathing and realize he was, in fact, alive. He rubbed his neck that still felt pain as he searched his room. He was alone; his door was still locked. It was a dream, he told himself. He felt reassured for just a moment until he remembered what his dreams of late had meant.

He glanced at the clock. Just after midnight. He needed to walk, to breathe in the fresh air. He wondered if he would run into Amarice again, wondered if she had had the same dream. Of course she had, he thought as he pulled on a shirt. This one felt far more real than the others. He grabbed his Scholar's pendant from his bedside table out of habit then thought better of it. A heavy chain seemed far too restrictive for his neck after the nightmare.

He unlocked his bedroom door and opened it into the cool midnight breeze that flowed through the corridor. He used his Gift to enhance his body heat and warm himself, then he walked into the courtyard. The moonlight reflecting on the water of the fountain was the only source of light tonight. He wandered slowly through the grass and evergreen trees, but Amarice was nowhere to be found. Maybe she slept soundly, and tonight's dream had no deeper meaning. He tried to convince himself of this, to no avail.

There was no use returning to his bedroom; his mind was far too awake to sleep. He found his way to the library and lit the fireplace. He feared what news would come in the next few days. He still did not understand why only he and Amarice had these dreams. There were other powerful Scholars in Elandria; it did not make sense for only him to share this connection to the Sage. He sighed. For now, he would lose himself in the words of others and worry about this dream tomorrow.

Quinn read in the library until pale yellow light crept through the windows. Yawning, he turned toward the clock; he had enough time to bathe and change before breakfast. Then he could discuss this dream with Amarice. But at this moment, all he wanted was several cups of coffee.

Amarice was not in the veranda when he entered, which was unusual. She was normally early to breakfast, chatting happily with Madge and the others. He took his seat and poured himself some coffee. Slowly, the rest of the Villa residents entered, some cheerful, others far less talkative. None of the Scholars had slept well, it seemed, but no one had the same dream. Quinn ate his eggs in silence. A half-hour passed, and Amarice still had not arrived. He considered going to find her, even though no one ever went to her personal chambers. Still, a knock to see if she was all right would not hurt. He mulled over this point and had nearly decided to go find her after breakfast, when she entered the veranda.

Her un-brushed hair had been pinned carelessly away from her face. She wore a wool shawl over her dress, unusual attire for the fashion-conscious Sage. Her eyes were red and puffy with dark circles underneath.

"You look terrible, Amarice," Daisy said.

"Thank you." Amarice's sarcasm stung this morning. She took her seat at the head of the table and met no one's eyes. She just sat, staring off into space. Everyone else chose to ignore her, except for Quinn. He poured her a cup of coffee. She nodded in thanks and downed the coffee in one swallow

He poured her another cup. "You should eat something. You'll feel better. I was up all night, too." She looked at his face and her lip quivered. "It's all right. We'll talk about it later." He spooned some eggs on her plate.

Amarice ate a few bites and finished her second cup of coffee. She did not speak until she rose from the table. "Come." Quinn followed her from the veranda through the ivy-lined walkway that led toward the river.

She walked slowly down the hill. The rush of the water grew louder as they drew nearer. Quinn noticed many of the trees had begun to turn greener. Spring was not far away. At the banks of the river, Amarice sat and stuck her feet in the icy water. The water slowed to a gentle pace, and, he knew, was probably quite warm from her magic. Quinn had no desire to follow suit; water was still an element with which he struggled. Instead he sat cross-legged next to her.

"Choking?" she asked. She seemed to struggle with sentences this morning. He nodded. She closed her eyes. He listened to her breath for a while. After some time, she spoke again. "It's been nearly two months." Quinn nodded again, unsure what to say. Several more minutes passed in silence. "There's nothing to do but wait for news, I suppose."

Quinn looked at her face. A single tear rolled down her cheek. He fought the desire to reach out and wipe it away. "Why us?" he asked her. She still had no answer for him. They continued to just sit on the banks, watching the river run, the fish jumping in and out of the water. The sun grew higher in the sky, kissing Quinn's face with warmth. The morning birds began their songs. For all the darkness of the night, the morning still rose lovely.

Amarice broke the silence. "There is a state dinner at the palace next week. A Lazori minister is coming to discuss the trade agreements with the king. Though I doubt the Lazori are behind these attacks, we mustn't rule out anything. The king believes they might be; or else, he wants to believe it." She paused and turned toward Quinn. "I'd like for you to come with me, to get your thoughts and intuitions on the matter."

A smile broke across Quinn's face, despite everything. His first diplomatic assignment—and dinner at the palace! He had never dreamed he would have the opportunity. And Amarice cared about his thoughts, his finely tuned intuition that came with the Gift of the Earth. "Of course," he said, far more composed than he felt. She smiled in return, some light returning to her eyes.

"You'll need to brush up on your knowledge of the Lazori."

He nodded. He recalled the basics: their superstitions, their tenuous relationship with Elandria, their deplorable practices of human slavery. It was the slavery that kept King Roland from establishing too many trade agreements with them. He would have banned all trade with Lazoria if he did not fear it would result in war. But recently, he had pushed Parliament to raise the tariffs on Lazori goods to discourage Elandrians from trade. The Lazori government was not happy.

"You should get some rest, Quinn, if your night was anything like mine. I think I'll return to bed. I'll let you know the minute I have news." She stood and touched his shoulder gently. He shivered at her touch. "Don't fear sleep." Amarice turned away and walked up the hill toward her chambers. A part of him wished he was going with her.

⚜

THAT MORNING, in a small town outside of Te'eh, a Messenger's screams woke the citizens. People rushed from their homes and businesses to see what was wrong.

There, on the tree that marked the town's center, a female Scholar hung. Her face was blue; it appeared she had been strangled by her own Scholar's pendant before being nailed to the tree. Her clothes had been stripped from her, and on her belly, the word "SIN" had been carved by a knife. Blood dripped and stained the grass below.

Hundreds of miles away, on the southern peninsula, one of the few remaining Deyoni camps sat, a flash of color on the winter-touched plain. No Deyoni rose this morning from their silken tents. Their fire burned untended, and the smell of burning flesh mingled with the cold breeze. Thirty burned corpses lay near the fire and would not be discovered for days.

CHAPTER 11

A marice laughed at Quinn's boyish excitement. He had spent most of the carriage ride down the mountain asking detailed questions about etiquette and expectations, nervous about getting anything wrong at the palace. "Relax, Quinn. King Roland will make you feel quite welcome." Quinn tried his hardest to relax but failed.

"Are you sure my clothes are appropriate?"

"No." He looked at her with wide eyes full of panic. "I think it best you just attend dinner naked." He blinked, then realized she was teasing him. He forced a nervous laugh. "You will be fine." He left her alone for a few minutes, and she mused on the prospect of him attending dinner at the palace without clothes. She hid her smile.

The carriage stopped at the base of the mountain for the horse to drink. Quinn climbed out to stretch; he did look cramped in the carriage with his height. Amarice stayed inside. She was not looking forward to the state dinner. She had heard rumors of the Lazori minister's repugnant personality, and recent events did not have her feeling overly diplomatic.

The latest attack had given some credence to the king's theory that the Lazori might be behind the attacks. Their rigid morality and degradation of women and slaves did not endear them to the Elandrians. Still, Amarice had her doubts. The people of Lazoria were highly suspicious of magic, but she had never heard of them viewing it as sinful. And the country's largest issue with Elandria was political in nature and did not concern the Scholars as a group. This latest Deyoni attack was at the farthest corner of Elandria from Lazoria. Her mind thought back to the slaughter of the Deyoni a few months' prior. She felt certain the attacks on the tribe and the burning of the forest were related to the deaths of the Scholars, and those did not seem likely to concern the rulers in Lazoria.

Quinn had mentioned that in his village earth magic and Deyoni were both viewed as sinful and degenerate. She knew many of the outlying villages held the same ideas and clung to various illogical religious traditions. But these attacks had happened all over Elandria, not in one isolated region. There were no major organized religions in Elandria to orchestrate these attacks. Perhaps dinner with the Lazori minister would give her some new insight into the cause. Or else prove I'm right, she thought bitterly.

The carriage door opened and Quinn took his seat across from Amarice. The carriage driver peered his head inside. "Do you wish to stop at the Deyoni camps, my lady?"

Amarice shook her head. "Not today. We will stop on our return journey." The driver nodded and shut the door. The horse began trotting southward to Teleah again. "Quinn, I have arranged for you to be seated near some of the Scholars of Parliament and a few of the Lazori traveling party. Listen for anything that might suggest the Lazori have knowledge of the attacks."

Quinn nodded. "You still do not think they will?"

"No, but we have no other leads. The king is highly suspicious of them, and rightfully so. But I do not think they are attacking our earth magic." She opened a book to read, ending the conversation. Quinn studied her face, admiring her beauty. Her mood shifted the nearer they drew to Teleah. She no longer emanated a presence of peace, but instead she seemed anxious. Her leg shook, a nervous tick he had never noticed.

After an hour or so, Quinn broke the silence. "Are you all right,

Amarice?" His voice was filled with concern. She looked up at him and smiled weakly.

"I loathe state dinners with foreign diplomats. I find them draining." She clutched her Scholar's pendant and stared out the window. Quinn saw a bit of himself in her at that moment. The Sage had no equals, and he had gathered over the last few months the role could be isolating. Amarice was a happy, vibrant woman, but the role of Sage required something else. Without looking back at Quinn, she murmured, "I'm glad you are with me for this one."

Quinn's heart lurched. He said nothing and stared out the window at the countryside. The farmland had turned a light shade of green since his trip to the Villa. He saw farmers preparing their fields for the early crops. Spring would be here soon.

The carriage approached the land just outside Teleah. He was shocked to see the camps of Deyoni had multiplied in the last few months. There were easily five thousand Deyoni or more residing on the outskirts of the capital. As the Sage's carriage passed them, many of the bronze-skinned nomads ran to the edge of the road to catch a glimpse of the magical woman inside.

"*Drabekesala! Drabekesala!*" they cried. Women threw flowers as the carriage passed. The men stood, solemn-faced, with their fists over their hearts in respect. The children ran after them. Amarice waved and smiled out her window. Cries of "*Drabekesala!*" followed them.

"What does it mean?" He was amazed by the love these strangers had for her, although he completely understood it. She was easy to love, and she was the Deyoni's greatest champion in Elandria.

"Roughly, 'magic earth mother,'" she replied with a laugh. "It loses something in translation, doesn't it?" She continued to wave out the window, speaking Deyoni to the children.

"They know you are half-Deyoni? I never knew until the Feast of Fire."

She nodded. "They know. I'm proud of my heritage, but it's not something I flaunt in my role as Sage. I hold much more sway with Parliament if I don't mention it. I don't hide it, but I don't draw attention to it either. Except at home." Quinn understood. Although she was the most powerful diplomat and the greatest Sage in history, discrimination of the Deyoni ran deep. Many of the ministers of Parliament came from smaller towns where the prejudice was much stronger. Even many of the Scholars still held some prejudice against the nomadic people, believing them ignorant. Amarice was smart to downplay her Deyoni side.

The Deyoni camps gave way to the parts of Teleah that rested outside the city walls. Amarice reached into her bag and pulled out a headpiece. The Sage's Diadem. Quinn had never seen her wear it. She placed it on her hair. The thin silver metal curved around her head, meeting in the center in the shape of a tree. Rubies, sapphires, emeralds, and diamonds lined the band across her forehead, representing fire, water, earth, and air.

She wore it well. The moment she placed the diadem on her head, her posture changed. She exuded an air of confidence and authority that she did not wear at the Villa. Quinn noticed the instant she transitioned from Amarice to Sage. If her earlier anxiety was still present, he could not see it. The woman before him was staggering. This was the Sage he had always imagined. This woman was the stuff of legends. He felt a sense of intimidation he had not felt since his arrival at the Villa two months prior.

The carriage passed through the city gates and ascended the hill toward the palace. Part of him expected there to be fanfare; the Sage deserved it. But her carriage was one of many on the road, and, if anyone noticed the Sage's symbol, they did not acknowledge it. Still, he believed she should be revered with cheers and trumpets.

Pulling his eyes away from the beautiful woman, Quinn looked out the window. He had never been this close to the palace, and now he was attending dinner and staying the night there. He could hardly believe what his life had become. The palace walls climbed into the sky, the same sparkling white stone of the Sage's Villa. Here, though, the towers reached several stories high. Marble balconies were scattered throughout the wide, arched windows. Massive gardens with landscaped hedges surrounded the vast palace. The carriage crossed the stone bridge that sat over the small Teleah River, and for the first time, Quinn could accurately experience the magnitude of the ancient architectural feat that stood before him. He gasped.

Amarice smiled at him. "Welcome to the palace of reigning King Roland, my dear apprentice." She let him marvel in silence until the horse stopped at the palace gates. "Let's get this over with, shall we?"

The driver opened the door and took the Sage's hand to escort her to the ground. Quinn exited behind her. He looked around: the giant city of Teleah seemed so small from the top of the hill. He could see the Academy at the foot of the hill, a collection of stone buildings that looked more like they were meant for dolls instead of humans. To the north, he could see the Sage's Mountains, hardly believing they were only a few hours' ride from where he stood. The palace seemed to shrink everything surrounding it.

Quinn followed the Sage through the three-story gates and into the hall where they were greeted by a butler. The butler bowed his head and pulled his hand to his brow in greeting. "My lady Sage." Amarice greeted him warmly and by name. Quinn noticed she did this to all the palace staff she encountered; even if she did not know their name, she greeted them as if they were old friends. Quinn could only smile and give short responses. He was too busy admiring the brightly painted murals and impressive construction illuminated by the sunlight that shone through the large stained-glass windows.

The butler led them to their rooms, and two attendants followed with Quinn and Amarice's belongings. They climbed several staircases before entering a large wing full of guest rooms. The butler stopped at two doors, side-by-side, and handed each of them a key before departing. Amarice unlocked the room to her door then turned to Quinn. "Get settled in and ready for dinner. The baths are down the hall to the right. Be ready in an hour and a half. I want to introduce you to the king before dinner. Find a maid if you get lost."

QUINN BATHED and dressed quickly then rested for a while in his room. He was glad to be out of the cramped carriage. He stretched out on the oversized bed with satin blankets and pillows. A small door led out to a balcony which provided him an overwhelming view of the gardens and, beyond, the early spring colors of the Teleah countryside.

After exactly an hour and a half, Quinn knocked on Amarice's door. "Come in," she yelled through the closed door.

Quinn entered tentatively, for she never allowed anyone in her bedroom at home. He found her standing near a full-sized mirror. He stopped short and gasped. In the mirror, he could see her from every angle. Her long black dress was a form-fitting velvet, accentuating her hips. Her breasts were in perfect form, and a keyhole in the neckline gave a subtle peek. He had the strong to desire to run his hands down the length of her exposed back..

She heard his gasp and turned to look at him. "What's the matter?"

"You're beautiful. I mean, I—Sorry." Amarice smiled. She turned her whole body toward him now to see him. His black, silk shirt tightened across his flat abdomen and muscular arms. To her delight, he wore his leather pants again, laces beckoning her gaze. She met his eyes; although his handsome face still had a boyish curve, he had changed. The confidence he had begun to build in his apprenticeship had turned him into a man.

"Don't apologize. You look great yourself. I'm almost ready." She turned back to the mirror and began fumbling with her diamond necklace. "Damn it!" She could not get the clasp to stay open long enough to fasten. "Can you put this necklace on me?" she asked, exasperated.

Quinn approached her, and he felt far more nervous than he should. It's just a necklace, he told himself. He stood behind her and took the ends of the necklace from her fingers. Their hands touched, and he tried to convince himself he had imagined the sparks. Amarice could feel his warm breath and soft hands. She ached to have him touch her, to put his arms around her. She inhaled deeply. Quinn took longer than he probably should have to fasten the necklace, but he did it. His hands grazed the back of her neck. She shivered.

He stepped back quickly, forcing himself to steady his breathing. They stood there wordlessly for a few moments, trying not to stare at each other. "Well," Amarice finally broke the heavy silence. "Are you ready to meet the king?"

QUINN FOLLOWED Amarice into a grand parlor. His nerves threatened to take over, both from his exchange with Amarice and the imminent moment in which he would meet the king of Elandria. He tried to calm himself, but watching Amarice's hips sway as she walked did nothing to help his thoughts. He sighed and focused on the back of her head instead.

The king's parlor was nothing short of ostentatious. Exquisitely carved marble columns reached to the domed ceiling where an incredible mural of the construction of Teleah was painted. The walls of the parlor had floral designs where they were not covered by heavy velvet tapestries. Candelabras glowed on fine wooden tables, next to oversized sofas upholstered in finest fabric. Quinn struggled to keep his jaw from dropping at the elaborate décor.

The Sage approached two men chatting near a side door, and Quinn realized one of them was the king. "Amarice!" the king exclaimed with a smile. The rotund man had a childlike grin set upon his dark face. What little hair remained on his head was greyish, contrasting with the elaborate golden crown he wore. His heavy brocade tunic of red and gold stretched tightly over his large belly. The other man, a few years older than Quinn, was short and muscular. His dark hair and caramel skin contrasted with his piercing, blue-green eyes. He, too, wore a heavy brocade, though in black. Quinn noticed a Scholar's pendant around his neck.

"My King." The Sage greeted him not with a bowed head but with a hug. "Prince Raymond," she said to other man. The prince kissed her cheek, lingering. Quinn felt a flash of emotion that he could not identify. "May I introduce my apprentice, Quinn Atwell?"

Quinn bowed his head in the customary manner. "Your highnesses, it is an honor." The prince nodded at Quinn, but the king smiled warmly.

"Amarice speaks highly of you," King Roland told him. Quinn's face grow hot in embarrassment. "I trust her completely, so I am honored to have you here. She tells me you are interested in a career in diplomacy?"

Quinn could only nod. The king began to tell him who would be at dinner tonight and promised to introduce him to as many people as he could. "Connections, my boy. It's all about connections." He gestured to Quinn to take a seat, and he began to ask Quinn questions about himself and his education. Quinn slowly relaxed in his presence.

Though it had been over a year since they had seen one another, Prince Raymond and Amarice rekindled their friendship in an instant, sharing stories of their travels and gossip about old friends from the Academy. They had studied together, and Quinn could not help but feel they had more of a history than just friends. Raymond was a kind man, funny and personable. However, there was something about him Quinn just did not like.

Others began entering the parlor, each greeting the king and the Sage in turn. As promised, King Roland introduced Quinn to everyone as the Sage's bright apprentice. Quinn tried to keep track of everyone's names. The Sage fulfilled her duty as the land's highest diplomat well. She greeted everyone with warmth and a sense of poise she normally did not carry at home. Quinn also could not help but notice that Raymond kept placing his hand on the small of Amarice's back. He pushed away thoughts of punching the prince in his perfect face. Amarice did not seem to mind his touch, and Quinn had no right to be jealous. Amarice belonged to herself, and herself alone. She could have anyone she wanted; indeed, she often did have whoever she wanted.

The Lazori minister and his traveling company entered the parlor, and everyone stopped to stare. They wore robes of silk dyed in browns and yellows. The minister had a formidable presence, and Quinn's instinct was that he did not like the man at all. The minister approached the king and nodded his head slightly. "King Roland," he said in a thick accent.

"Minister Kaspar." There was no love lost between these two men. The room had grown quiet, absorbing the tension. "May I introduce Amarice Teyvana, the Sage of Elandria?"

The minister held out his hand, so Amarice extended hers. The Lazori took her hand and kissed it, far too long with impure intentions. A look of disgust crossed Amarice's face, and she withdrew her hand from his. "My lady. Rumors of your beauty travel far and wide."

"I hope those are not the only rumors you have heard about me,"

Amarice retorted, the smile plastered on her face not matching the ice in her voice.

"Forgive me. It is unusual for me to see women in political gatherings. We normally keep our women at home with the children or to warm our beds." He winked at her.

The king, the prince, and Quinn all gaped at the man's presumption, all ready to jump to her defense. But the Sage of Elandria did not need a man to fight her battles. She spoke again. "Unfortunate. I keep myself wherever I so please."

She silenced the sleazy Lazori for the moment. He nodded toward Raymond. "Prince, how nice to see you again." His tone suggested it was anything but nice. The prince greeted him appropriately, but did not mask the disdain in his voice.

A bell rang, signaling dinner. The doors to the dining room opened. Amarice smiled at Quinn before following the king to the head of the table. Quinn entered with the rest of the guests to find his seat.

He had never seen a table so large. The state dining room seated fifty people easily. Attendants lined the walls, pitchers and platters in hand. Quinn found his name on a place card next to a Scholar from Parliament and across from several Lazori. The rest of the Lazori were far more pleasant than the minister. Indeed, he gathered they did not care for the man, either. They asked Quinn and the other Scholar many questions about earth magic, but their voices only suggested curiosity, not suspicion.

Quinn scanned the table, looking for Amarice. She sat at the left-hand side of the king, a greater position of honor than even the prince sat. Opposite her sat the Lazori minister, in the seat typically reserved for the guest of honor. Prince Raymond sat on Amarice's other side, focusing intently on every word Amarice said. The image of punching him popped into Quinn's mind again; he drank more wine.

Dinner was uneventful. Course after course of meats and vegetables and pastries was served. It was delicious, but Quinn noticed Amarice had been right—Madge's cooking at the Villa was superior. The wine, however, was the richest and sweetest he had ever drunk. He listened to the conversations around him, waiting for any hint that the Lazori might be behind the attacks in Elandria. Mostly, though, the foreigners were amicable and interesting. He wondered if a handful of men like Minister Kaspar gave the entire country a bad reputation before he remembered their practice of slavery.

After dinner, the guests retired to the parlor once again. The king, grateful to get away from Kaspar, found Quinn and introduced him to several more people. Amarice mingled with the guests, catching Quinn's eye occasionally and smiling. Usually Prince Raymond would appear whenever she did and divert her attention.

The Lazori minister approached Quinn. "You are the Sage's apprentice?" he asked. Quinn answered with as much respect as he could muster. "Interesting. In Lazoria, we do not accept teachings from women."

"That's a shame," Quinn replied. "I find women have much to teach us." He felt a hand at his elbow. Amarice. She smiled sweetly at Kaspar, who walked away without a word. "I don't like him," Quinn told her.

"No one does. How has your evening gone? I'm sorry I had to abandon you, but you seemed to be fine."

Quinn looked down at the woman before him. Her grey eyes sparkled in the candlelight. "It's been wonderful." She flashed her best smile at Quinn, pride and affection on her face. He had come a long way in the last few months. He let himself feel a bit of pride about his own growth.

Prince Raymond appeared and placed his hand on Amarice's back. Quinn stifled a sigh of exasperation. Raymond was friendly, a genuinely likeable man. He treated Quinn with respect and interest, yet Quinn kept imagining him falling down a flight of stairs. The three of them shared stories of the Academy as the crowd slowly dwindled to a select few.

"Raymond," the king called, and gestured for his son to follow him. Raymond bid Amarice and Quinn goodnight.

Sage and apprentice made their way upstairs to their guestrooms. Amarice yawned. "I'm exhausted. I don't know why sitting in a carriage doing nothing is so tiring, but it is." She unlocked her door. "Good-night, Quinn. Sweet dreams." She disappeared into her room.

"They will be," he whispered. He undressed and lay in the oversized palace bed. He fell asleep smiling, thinking of Amarice in her black dress.

◎✦◎

A KNOCK on the door woke Quinn from his dreams. He squinted at the clock. Nearly three o'clock in the morning. He groaned as he pulled himself from the bed and answered the door.

Amarice stood before him, dressed in a gauzy white nightgown that left little to the imagination, a velvet cloak draped over her arm. She looked magical, framed by the moonlight. For a moment, Quinn let himself be hopeful.

She stared at her gorgeous apprentice. He wore only linen pants, his bare chest slender and chiseled. She reached a hand out as if to touch him, then pulled it back, aware of herself again. She cleared her throat. "The king requests an audience with us."

Quinn's heart fell. "Now?" he asked, confusion and disappointment in his voice.

"He wants to know our thoughts before his meeting with Kaspar in the morning." She studied Quinn a little longer before fastening her cloak around her. "Put on a shirt." More for my sake than the king's, she thought. Quinn grabbed his shirt and followed Amarice to the king's study.

The king sat behind a large oak desk. Quinn was disappointed to see Prince Raymond seated on a leather sofa. Amarice closed the door behind them then took a seat next to the prince. Quinn stayed standing by the door. "Well?" the king asked. "Thoughts?"

Amarice turned toward Quinn. "Quinn, what do you think?"

Quinn was taken aback. Here he was in the king's study in the middle of the night, and he had been asked his thoughts about the Lazori company. His mind still foggy with sleep, he tried his hardest not to make a fool of himself. "I don't like Kaspar." They all stared at him, waiting for him to continue. Stupid, he thought. No one likes Kaspar. He searched his brain for a coherent thought. "It seems most of his company do not like him either. They were friendly and not suspicious toward earth magic. They knew nothing of the attacks. I don't think Kaspar is behind it, although he is a deplorable man."

Amarice nodded. "I concur. He just wants to amend the trade deals, likely for personal gain. But he is, as Quinn said, deplorable."

The king nodded. "Then who is behind the attacks?" No one spoke. No one had an answer. "Very well. Amarice, should I increase trade with Lazoria? Parliament has said they will support whatever I decide."

Amarice looked thoughtful. "Unfortunately, I think the answer is yes. While that man—" her voice was filled with disgust— "sits so close to the king of Lazoria, we need to do whatever we can to keep peace." Quinn saw Raymond place his hand on Amarice's knee.

King Roland sighed. "I knew you would say that. You're right, as always. Thank you for coming at this late hour. Go back to sleep, or whatever it is you do in the middle of the night." The Sage and the prince ducked their heads. "I may not be a Scholar," the king continued. "But I do recognize the lust of young people. You have been eyeing one another all evening." Quinn's heart dropped into his stomach.

Quinn followed the prince and Amarice back to the guest rooms. "Goodnight, Quinn," she told him. Was that a hint of regret in her voice? Surely, he imagined it. He wished her goodnight, and she disappeared into her room with Prince Raymond.

Quinn opened the door to his balcony and stepped out into the moonlight to breathe in the cool night air. The door to the balcony next to him opened, and he heard Raymond's voice from inside the room. "I'm surprised it's me warming your bed tonight and not your apprentice." Quinn's breath left him. He should not eavesdrop, but he stayed rooted to his spot.

"What on earth do you mean?"

"Don't play dumb with me. I know you better than that." There was a long pause. "He's in love with you. And I think..."

Amarice cut him off. "Don't be ridiculous. Are you going to get undressed or what?"

Raymond laughed. "Fine. I have missed you. It's been hard finding an adequate lover on my travels."

"Oh, I'm sure you've been struggling terribly." The prince laughed again, and Quinn went inside. He did not want to hear any more of their exchange. He lay on the satin sheets and folded his arms behind his head, thinking.

In love with the Sage. He had not wanted to admit it to himself, had not wanted to give credence to those thoughts. It was irrational. She would never love him back, would she? He thought back through the evening. He wondered if she had felt the same spark of desire when he helped her with her necklace. And had she nearly touched his bare chest earlier when she knocked on his door? What was Raymond going to say before she cut him off, calling him ridiculous?

Quinn groaned with frustration. Amarice was the Sage. He was her apprentice, a fifth-year Scholar student with no life experience. She could have anyone she wanted, and she was wanted by everyone. Despite only being two years younger than her, Quinn was a boy. Amarice was the most powerful woman who had ever lived. She was not his to love.

CHAPTER 12

The next morning dawned bright and warm. Quinn shared a breakfast with Amarice and a handful of other guests in a smaller dining room. He did not see the king or Prince Raymond. Amarice was friendly, but Quinn was not talkative. She assumed he was tired from the late-night meeting and the day of travel, so she did not push him.

They shared a carriage ride into the main part of the city. Amarice had plans with an old friend from school, and Quinn had arranged to meet Rafe for lunch. Jack's crotchety apothecary master would not let him attend. Quinn still had little to say.

"Are you well, Quinn?" she asked, concerned.

He nodded, but he did not say anything. After a while, he became overcome with curiosity and could not keep himself from asking Amarice an immensely personal question. "You and the prince..." His voice trailed off, thinking better of it. Amarice sighed.

"We were together in school. That's how I know the king so well; our relationship is deeper than Sage and King. Roland is like the father I never knew. But Raymond..." She thought for a while. "He wanted me to marry him, but I had no desire to become a princess or, later, a queen. The Sage is who I am meant to be. And I never, well, I never loved him as deeply as he loved me. I keep telling myself he no longer loves me, that it's all in good fun, but I'm not sure." She gave a sad laugh. "You probably think I'm cruel to keep inviting him to my bed. Perhaps I am."

"You couldn't be cruel if you tried," Quinn whispered. Amarice looked at him, her grey eyes watering. She opened her mouth to speak when the carriage stopped. The driver opened the door.

"We're here, sir."

Quinn looked outside and saw the familiar facade of Bucky's Tavern, the smells of the city on the breeze. He smiled at Amarice wistfully and left the carriage. He watched her drive away and forced himself to regain his composure. He was, after all, excited to see his best friend. He entered the brightly lit tavern.

The dark-skinned barkeep greeted him happily, hugging him and shoving a pint of ale into his hand. Quinn laughed, pleased to see the kind older man. He turned to look for Rafe. His old roommate stood upon seeing him. "Quinn!" Rafe threw his arms around him. "I've missed you, friend." He pointed at a seat near the window. Quinn sat.

"I've missed you, too." He sipped the ale. "What is new in Teleah?"

Rafe filled him in on the latest gossip. He rarely saw Jack, whose apprenticeship kept him busy with little time for fun. "He has plans to put the old bastard out of business the second his apprenticeship is done." Apparently, the customers much preferred Jack's bedside manner—Quinn could understand that. Sarah no longer hated Quinn, as she had met a Scholar at the hospital who had her smitten. He told him about their other friends and the professors. "Viridion is a strange man, but he's amazing," Rafe told him. "I've learned so much."

Bucky brought out two bowls of stew and a loaf of bread. Quinn filled him in on his apprenticeship, trying to control the emotion in his voice when he spoke of Amarice. He focused instead on his studies and the meetings with various visitors. He told him about dinner at the palace last night.

Rafe gave his friend an appraising look. "You've changed."

Quinn swirled his bread in his stew. "Well, I can actually do earth magic now, without causing a natural disaster." He took a bite.

His friend shook his head. "No, you're more... something. More confident, more at peace with yourself." Rafe finished off his ale and beckoned to Bucky for a refill. "I'm glad. I worried about you the last four years. I don't know what darkness lies in your past, but you finally seem happy and comfortable."

Quinn shifted; despite his newfound confidence, he still felt uncomfortable talking about himself like this. Rafe meant well, but he did not have the same reassuring presence as Amarice. But Rafe was the first person who ever felt like family to Quinn. "One day, I'll tell you all about me," he promised his friend.

Rafe nodded, not pushing the subject. He told Quinn he had been spending time in the Deyoni camps after receiving Quinn's letter about their magic. "It's different from ours, but it's there. I'm not sure how to describe it. They just seem to be one with the earth." Quinn told him in more detail about the dance at the Feast of Fire and mentioned the Sage's mother was Deyoni. Rafe had no idea, as he had expected.

They finished their lunch. "I'm going with Viridion's group to Seluya," he told Quinn. "We're going to help regrow the forest. The damage is immense, and the Scholars there need help."

"Good, they need people like you, Rafe."

They hugged before parting ways. Quinn was sad to see his friend go, but was happy he had found his niche. He knew Rafe would do great things with his earth magic. He smiled and began the walk back to the palace.

He stopped in the apothecary shop to see Jack on his way up the hill. The small shop was nestled between a brothel and a pub, but it had been here long before. There were many apothecaries in Teleah, but none were as famous as this old one with its cracking blue paint and worn sign.

When he entered, Jack was helping an older woman at the counter. "Not only will this stop the pain, Gerta, but you'll be much more limber." He winked, and the grey-haired matron giggled like a schoolgirl. She paid him and bustled out the door. Quinn shook his head. Same old Jack.

"Quinn!" His friend hurried into the main part of the shop. "I did not know you were stopping by!"

They hugged and chatted for a few minutes. "I don't have long before the bastard yells at me to get back to work," Jack explained. He told Quinn in a hushed voice that he had already memorized all the tinctures, perfected several, and was simply biding his time until the year was over. The apothecary master only took on apprentices to get cheap workers to deal with the customers. He had no desire to teach or discuss the science with Jack.

"You'll put him out of business in a year," Quinn told him.

"I hope so. Old git."

A new customer entered the shop, so the friends said goodbye. Quinn finished his walk through the wide main street to the palace. He found he did not miss the bustle and crowds of the city. He returned through the gates and spent the rest of the afternoon in quiet meditation in the palace gardens.

※

QUINN ENTERED the carriage the next morning before Amarice, anxious to return to the Villa. He looked out the carriage window at the Sage, who looked even more dazzling in the morning light glinting off the palace walls. She bade farewell to King Roland and Prince Raymond. The prince leaned in to kiss her farewell, and she turned her head quickly before climbing in the carriage. Or perhaps Quinn imagined it.

She smiled at Quinn. "I'm ready to go home. Ready to become Amarice again, and to sleep in my own bed."

Quinn returned her smile. "I agree, except for the part about the bed. I barely fit in mine." He laughed, the awkwardness of yesterday subsiding. He may not be the Sage's lover, but he could certainly enjoy his time learning from her. She laughed, too, joking about his gargantuan height. They chatted a bit about the Lazori company, and she asked him how his lunch with Rafe had gone.

The carriage passed through the city gates into the surrounding town. "I hope you don't mind a slight delay, Quinn. I'd like to stop at the Deyoni camps on our way to the mountain." He assured her that he would not mind at all, and the prospect of at last seeing the Deyoni up close excited him. As the horse trotted nearer to the camps, he inquired of Amarice the proper greetings and customs for meeting the Deyoni. "If they give you a show, pay them in coin. Dancing, fire-eating, anything. But do not offer them coin unless they have worked for it. They are a proud people; they do not take kindly to handouts." Quinn nodded and fished his coin purse from his bag, affixing it to his belt.

The driver halted the horse in the heart of the Deyoni's camps. Crowds of Deyoni pushed forward to see the Sage, their *Drabekesala*. Amarice climbed down amongst the hordes of people, greeting them all in fluent Deyoni. Their brightly colored garments contrasted with great beauty against their bronze skin. Their smiles were wide. Quinn descended the steps of the carriage warily. The Deyoni studied him with interest. Amarice told them something and gestured toward Quinn, and then they began to greet him happily. Two young children grabbed Quinn's hands and pulled him through the crowd. Amarice, too, was guided by two girls; she looked back at Quinn and laughed. "They accept you, my dear apprentice!"

The crowds broke into a circle, and the children beckoned for Quinn and Amarice to sit on two woven carpets on the grass. They obliged. Three men in green vests and tattooed chests rushed forward with drums. They began to beat a fast-paced rhythm, as three women in traditional garb stepped out of the crowd to dance, their skirts swirling rainbows. The air buzzed as they dance, and Quinn once again felt the deepest magic of the earth fill his soul. This dance, though, was not a feeling of fire that cleansed him of grief. The dance filled him with an immense happiness, such as he had never felt before. He felt himself laughing, although he felt disconnected from his body.

The dancing women pulled Amarice from the ground, despite her half-hearted protests. She joined their dance, never missing a step. She twirled and swayed, bouncing her hips with the beat of the drums. Her face reflected the late-morning sun. Quinn believed wholeheartedly that nothing more beautiful had ever come from this world than the woman dancing before him.

The music stopped as suddenly as it started. Amarice pulled a still-dazed Quinn to his feet, as the crowd pushed in for a chance to speak with the Sage. "Give them coin," she murmured. He nodded and gave each of the performers a generous sum.

Their progress back to the carriage was slowed as the men, women, and especially children pushed each other out of the way to see Amarice. Quinn followed a half-pace behind her, laughing as the children requested to be lifted to his "giant view." He picked them each up in turn. Amarice's eyes sparkled as she watched her apprentice. Quinn could no longer understand why the Deyoni were viewed with suspicion; they were a welcoming people, and there was nothing evil about them.

All of a sudden, Quinn stopped abruptly. A tall Deyoni man had made his way through the crowd, and he stood directly in front of Amarice. Despite his bronze skin and age, it was like looking in a mirror. He met Quinn's eyes and froze. Never before had Quinn seen someone who resembled him so much; indeed, he looked little like his family back home, save his mother's hair color. The Deyoni man noticed it, as well. Quinn pushed closer through the throngs of people.

Amarice glanced up at Quinn's face, feeling her apprentice's change in mood. She furrowed her brow in confusion and followed his gaze to the man standing in front of her. The resemblance was uncanny.

The man spoke. "Eleanor."

"What did you say?" Quinn's tone was nearly a shriek. "What did you say?"

But the hordes of people had pushed the man out of the way. Quinn tried to follow him. "What did you say?" he exclaimed over and over. The ground began to tremble beneath his feet. "What did you say?"

The Deyoni screamed at the trembling of the earth. "QUINN!" Amarice shouted. He did not look at her, but kept pushing through the crowd looking for the man. Amarice forced the ground to steady, not an easy task. Quinn's emotions were strong. "Quinn!" She grabbed his arm from behind him. "Quinn, he's gone. Come, let's go back to the carriage."

She led him back and pushed him in the carriage, climbing in after him. She waved out the window at the Deyoni while keeping her eyes on her apprentice. He was white as a sheet, his breathing rapid and irregular. The horse pulled the carriage past the camps quickly. She gave him a few minutes to collect himself before speaking.

"Quinn, speak to me. Are you well?"

He turned his face to meet hers but seemed to look through her. "That man. Did you see that man?" His voice quivered.

"Yes, he looked just like you. Who is Eleanor?"

Quinn swallowed, and for the first time since entering the carriage looked directly in the Sage's eyes. "Eleanor is my mother. Amarice, I think that man is my father."

CHAPTER 13

Amarice left Quinn alone for several days to process this latest revelation. If he showed up to meals, he was silent. Often, she would see him wandering the grounds or running along the river. She hoped this would not prove a setback in the progress he had made with harnessing the power of his Gift.

Quinn had written multiple drafts of letters to his mother. The tones ranged from sad to matter-of-fact to angry. Yet he sent none of them. Though he was angry and struggling with his identity, so much of his childhood made sense. He never looked like his blond-haired, blue-eyed father and brother. His father never seemed to love him the way he loved Corbin, Quinn's younger brother. And though it was rumored that a Scholar had existed in his mother's family tree, he was the first person in Corthy with the Gift of the Earth in generations.

He crumpled up the latest letter he had written and sighed. His mother. She was kind and loving, but she had always wished for Quinn to fit in with the rest of the village. She never seemed angry when his Gift ran wild, though. Sad, but never angry. Eleanor was far less religious than Quinn's father—or, Quinn thought bitterly, the man he had called father—but she was the most adamant that Quinn never see the Deyoni when they set up camp near Corthy. He had always assumed it was the same fear and suspicion that fueled everyone else's discrimination. Now he wondered if his mother had feared Quinn would discover the truth.

Writing these letters was unproductive, so Quinn left his room to go for another run along the river. There he let his emotions flow into the banks and the water. As the river sped faster and faster with his turbulence, he ran faster, too. It had been three days since he had returned to the Villa. He missed Amarice, although he appreciated her not pushing him to talk.

He returned to his room, dripping in sweat, and pushed open the door. He stopped in the doorway, gaping. While he was gone, his small, single bed had been replaced with a large, double bed. There was less room between the bed and desk now, but this new bed was much more appropriately sized for a young man over six feet tall. He smiled to himself.

"Do you like it? We can move you to a bigger room if you'd prefer." A melodic voice rang behind him. He turned and saw Amarice standing there, grinning.

"It's wonderful. Thank you."

"I wish I had known sooner," she told him. "I often don't think of these details. This has always been the apprentice's room, but I believe you might be the tallest Sage's apprentice ever." She grinned.

He stepped toward her, as if to embrace her, but stopped short. The air between them grew tense. They simply stared at one another for several moments, before Amarice broke the silence. "It's time for you to stop brooding. The fact that you are, it appears, half-Deyoni, is great news for us." He furrowed his brow, confused. She smiled and explained. "You see, I've been poring through the writings of all the past Sages looking for something about dream magic. I just have not understood why you and I keep having these dreams. But I've been looking in the wrong place. We need to be looking for answers in the Deyoni." She continued, explaining that she believed dreams must have played a role in causing all the nomadic tribes to venture toward the cities they hated and set up semi-permanent camp. After all, there had been only two attacks on their people, but they came to the cities by the thousands.

"I have sent word asking for the Deyoni shamans to come to the Villa for the Sage's Sabbath. I hope they will. But until then, I need your help, Quinn. We need to find anything we can about dream magic in the volumes about the Deyoni."

❦

QUINN THREW himself wholeheartedly into their research. Could the thing, unknown for so long, that had made Quinn such an outsider give him a purpose? Sage and apprentice spent hours reading in the library, stacks of books growing ever taller. Unfortunately, most of the writings on the Deyoni gave little mention of their magic. The histories were biased against these ancient people.

"I'll just write my own damn book about the Deyoni!" Quinn exclaimed one afternoon, throwing the latest unhelpful book on the floor. "If I read one more page about how ignorant and savage they are..." A torrent of warm wind blew through the open windows and ruffled the pages of several open tomes. Quinn raised a hand to calm the wind. "Sorry." He could not always control nature's reactions to his anger, but at least he now knew how to stop it from getting out of control.

"You should," Amarice said, brushing her wind-blown hair from her face.

"Should what?"

"Write your own damn book. Think of how far-reaching an unbigoted, comprehensive study of Deyoni magic would be. Think of the implications for Scholars and their Gifts."

Quinn pondered this idea. Could he do it? Could he write a book that would improve both the lives of the tribal people and the magic of the Scholars? He would have to consider this more, later. Maybe this was where his career would take him. Maybe he could help Amarice shape the future of these people—his people. But they weren't his people, not really. He may never see the man from the crowd again. And he was just a young Scholar with dreams of grandeur. His old friend self-doubt crept into his mind.

Then he looked at Amarice. She believed he could do it. He saw it on her face. Amarice had a way of making anything seem possible. This woman, the most powerful woman in the world, believed in him. He grinned at her.

⁜

DESPITE HIS NEWFOUND CONFIDENCE, their research proved largely unhelpful. New books were delivered almost daily to the Villa. Occasionally, one of them would stumble across a brief mention of Deyoni dream prophets, but the books either provided no more than a sentence or two or cited an individual who had been dead for centuries.

The weather grew warmer and the shades of winter shifted in pale greens. Every morning looked like a soft watercolor painting, and Quinn had taken to waking early to take a run at sunrise. One such morning, he returned sweating and panting to find Amarice standing outside his bedroom door. His heart leaped into his throat with a glint of hope. She looked him over, and he felt wildly self-conscious of his current state of appearance.

"How on earth do you wake up so early to run? I try to stay in bed as long as possible."

He laughed. "I like being out when the sun rises. So, what are you doing awake this early then?"

Amarice said nothing for a while, as if she were unsure herself why she stood at Quinn's door before breakfast. She opened her mouth to speak once or twice then closed it without a word. Quinn studied her curiously. She glowed in the pale morning light, her eyes still full of sleep. She lacked her normal finesse and confidence; yet, she was exquisite. Finally, she spoke. "We have not done much earth magic of late, sequestered away in the library. I was hoping you would take a walk with me."

She led him out of the Villa and through the northern gardens. They passed the Consort's Tree, which had stayed in full bloom since Quinn's wild magic had revived it. Quinn smiled. That seemed so long ago, but it had been barely three months. He had arrived in the heart of winter; now the first day of spring was right around the corner.

Amarice led him down the slope of the mountain, toward the area where she had burned and revitalized the earth. Finally, she sat in the grass, as if this random spot had been exactly what she was looking for. Perhaps it was. She gestured to Quinn to sit across from her. He sat, and she closed her eyes.

The air was still and the morning dew still dampened the ground. Far enough from the nearest woods, the stillness was uninterrupted by birds. Quinn let the earth's magic fill him until he felt warm and strong. The Sage sat quietly, breathing in the life of the morning. She stayed quiet so long, her voice startled him when she spoke.

"Do you feel at peace?" she asked him. He nodded. "One of the most powerful uses of the Gift of the Earth is to change the feeling of a room. I want you to change the air. Create a space of peace and safety."

"I don't know how."

"You do, you just haven't figured it out yet. Go on." She closed her deep grey eyes again, giving him no further instruction. *What is that supposed to mean?* He wondered. *I have no clue what I'm supposed to do.* Still, Amarice had never led him astray. He trusted her, so he tried to push away his self-doubt. He closed his eyes.

He sat for a long time, letting the earth's magic flow through him. He placed his bare hands on the wet ground to strengthen his connection. Time passed; he was unsure how long. He tried not to think about what to do. *Peace and safety.* As he thought it, he imagined a pale blue light surrounding him. Or perhaps, it was real. He did not know. *Peace and safety.* There it was again, only when his eyes were closed.

Quinn focused all his attention on this strange blue light. He realized it wasn't surrounding him, but was a part of him. He took note of his body; he could no longer feel the coolness of the morning, the dampness of the ground. Only the blue light. It was neither hot nor cold; it was intangible, but it was a part of him. The longer he focused on it, the more he felt that it was real. Invisible with open eyes, but as real as the woman sitting in front of him.

Realization dawned on him. If the light was a part of him, could he control it? He concentrated as hard as he could. He forced the blue light to grow, to extend past him like an extra limb. It worked! He pictured Amarice sitting in front of him and pushed the light toward her. It took a strength he had not anticipated, and he could feel his Gift surging through him as if it were frantically running. He pushed harder. The light reached her. He pushed it further, his magic leaving him. The light spread over Amarice, enveloping her in its protective aura.

He opened his eyes. The light was gone, as was the feeling of peace and safety he had controlled. He gasped, weak. Had he imagined it?

Amarice grinned. "You did it!"

His eyes widened. "I did? You saw it?"

She shook her head. "No, only you can see it. And every person sees something different; some people see a bubble, some people a shield or a curtain. But I felt it, before you dropped it. The air had a slight buzz, but I felt peaceful and protected when it touched me." Quinn had so many questions, but he felt so weak. "Replenish yourself," she told him, sensing his thoughts. "We'll talk more, later."

They sat in silence for a time longer. Quinn pulled the magic, the ever-sustaining Gift of the Earth, into himself. He had never used so much power. As he felt the earth's magic again, he let himself feel proud.

He asked her many questions as they walked slowly back toward the Villa. She assured him that with practice, it would become quicker and less draining. She said the audible buzzing would go away the more he did it, that most Scholars never practice this enough to get rid of the noise. She told him he could use it to bring happiness to a place of grief, respect to a place of dishonor, and peace to a place of turmoil.

They passed the Consort's Tree again and walked through the stone arch of the northern gardens. "Amarice?" She met his eyes, waiting for him to continue. "If every Scholar sees something different, what do you see?"

She smiled, as she turned toward her quarters. "A pale blue light."

A MESSENGER ARRIVED at lunchtime with a letter for the Sage. It was an update from the Chief Inquisitor. Amarice pulled Quinn into her study to discuss the latest news.

A growing suspicion of magic existed in the outlying towns. Inquisitors reported hearing village folk blaming Scholars and Deyoni for small issues—everything from stolen loaves of bread to the pro-Deyoni laws of Parliament. In town meetings, discontent with forest protection laws abounded. Some villagers blamed those laws, and by proxy the Scholars, for their inability to extend their land and towns. The small religious sects in the outskirts of Elandria began preaching more and more about the unnaturalness of the Scholars' gift.

Amarice thought that was hilarious. "The whole idea of our magic is that it is completely natural; we can't do anything without a connection to the natural world." She shook her head at the ignorance.

The letter had included an example of the propaganda seen in the villages. All across the outer regions of Elandria, posters with the same message had been placed around village squares and near churches: "Resist the Sinners' Sorcery." Not all the villagers bought into these ideas; most who had ever directly encountered Scholars had no qualms with their power. These villagers reported, over pints of ale, an influx of travelers with loud opinions. Always men, always alone, never with a clear destination.

The negative sentiments in some villages had grown so severe that many Scholars who made their homes there—schoolteachers, apothecaries, healers—had left and returned to the cities. If the pattern continued, there would be a shortage of positions available soon. Amarice made a note to contact the Academy. She could house some Scholars, but the Academy would need to take in others. Scholars did not turn their backs on one another in times of hardship, and many would take in their homeless brethren. But the Sage and the Academy could afford to house and provide some income to those without work. In the meantime, she and the Academy would need to produce something to counter the propaganda.

CHAPTER 14

The Villa greeted many guests over the next few days. With this newest information from the Royal Inquisitors, the Sage had requested the audience of many people. The High Inquisitor and several members of Parliament came to discuss the safety of the Scholars and the Deyoni. Quinn enjoyed watching Amarice command these meetings. Though she respected every person's input and respected the ancient tradition of democracy, it was clear that she was the real force in the proceedings. She managed to be kind but adamant. And though the king typically deferred his power to Parliament, with the peace in Elandria threatened, everyone knew the Sage had the king's ear. What Amarice wanted is what would happen.

The next crowd of guests were the professors who ran the Academy: Quickthorn, Viridion, and Metrarch. Professor Quickthorn greeted Quinn amicably. "You've changed," she told him. "Do you still doubt your power?" Quinn just smiled.

Amarice led the meeting in her study. Though together the three professors and the Sage comprised the official leadership of the Scholars in Elandria, and the Sage held the most power, Amarice still treated her former professors with great reverence. Quinn sat near the corner of the study; he felt unqualified to be there. Indeed, he wondered if he would be allowed in any of these meetings if he did not have the same dreams as the Sage.

"How much room does the Academy have for Scholars who need a home?" Amarice asked the professors.

"It would be quite cramped," Professor Viridion answered in his high-pitched voice, "but we determined we can house seventy-five. We can afford salaries for one hundred, though."

Quickthorn added, "That figure does include the thirty that have already returned."

The Sage nodded. "I can house and pay twenty to join us at the Villa. We'll need to reach out to the well-established Scholars in Teleah to see who can open up rooms or find work for them. If the influx continues, I expect we'll have several hundred over the next few months."

Viridion offered to take on that responsibility. Metrarch said he would recruit students to help create pro-Scholar literature to disseminate to the outer villages. "We'll also reach the inner villages preemptively."

"And pro-Deyoni literature?" Amarice asked. The professors shifted uncomfortably. No one spoke. Though the professors were not strictly anti-Deyoni, they held many of the same biases that the common folk did. For the first time since they arrived, Amarice gave them a look that clearly said I am the Sage, and I'm asking for your solutions. Quickthorn began playing with the rings on her fingers. Viridion stared intently at the nearest tapestry. Metrarch simply sat stone-faced.

"I'll do it," Quinn piped up quietly. They all turned to look at the young apprentice. He met Amarice's eyes, and she beamed at him. "I'll create it if the Academy will print and disseminate it." Amarice gave an appraising look at the professors, and they nodded emphatically.

"Excellent," the Sage said. "I think we're done here. I will see you all at dinner." The professors stood to excuse themselves. Quinn began to follow them out of the study. "Quinn, you should stay." He nodded and shut the door after the professors. The second they were gone, Amarice dropped her Sage persona with a groan, and Quinn relaxed. He collapsed in the seat across from her desk and shook his head. "Thank you," she told him.

He shrugged. "I just don't understand." But he did—the Deyoni never integrated themselves into mainstream society. Their ways were different, and humans by nature feared different. However, the professors were Scholars, the ones who preached knowledge above all else. There was so much to learn from these societal outcasts, if one only put forth the effort.

Sage and apprentice spent the next several hours planning how best to send pro-Deyoni messages. Quinn thought he could easily spend the rest of his life in Amarice's presence, planning, reflecting, and laughing. If only Amarice felt the same, he thought. He pushed the thoughts away; he had a mission now.

❧

TWO DAYS LATER, as the Villa prepared in earnest for the Sage's Sabbath, three Deyoni shamans arrived. Two elderly women in vibrant skirts entered the Villa gracefully, their hair wrapped in silken scarves, faces decorated with jewels. A short man, old enough to be Quinn's grandfather, followed two steps behind, in flared pants and an open vest of blue velvet. He wore a sash around his waist.

Quinn felt unexpectedly disappointed. Part of him had hoped one of the shamans would be the man who so resembled him. Improbable, he knew, considering the thousands of Deyoni camped outside of Teleah. But he had wanted to meet this man, to ask him about his mother, about his heritage.

"*Drabekesala!*" they greeted Amarice with warm embraces. Amarice chatted with them in the courtyard in their language, before switching to the common tongue.

"Meet my apprentice, Quinn Atwell." She gestured toward Quinn, who bowed in reverence. The man bowed in return, as did one of the women. The other, shriveled with a bird-like face, eyed him up and down.

"He is Deyoni." Her accent was thick, but her message was unmistakable. Quinn and Amarice both looked at the woman in surprise, then looked at each other. Quinn gaped; he had no words.

Amarice spoke in his stead. She could not hide the shock in her voice at the elderly shaman's appraisal. "Well, we believe he is half Deyoni. We saw a man who resembled him and knew his mother, but we did not get a chance to speak with him."

"It is in his heart." The woman finally bowed to Quinn. "Welcome, brother. We accept you." Quinn stuttered out words of thanks, unsure if he was coherent or not. The woman turned to the other two and muttered something in Deyoni.

Quinn looked at Amarice questioningly. She looked puzzled and shook her head. Maybe she had not heard what they said. Amarice turned to lead the shamans to their meeting. He expected her to take them into the study, but she walked past the courtyard and into the northern gardens. The shamans followed silently as she led them past the Consort's Tree and down the hill. She walked to the spot where she had taught Quinn much of his magic and sat in the grass.

With an adeptness uncharacteristic of people their age, the shamans sat on the grass, forming a small circle with Amarice. Quinn took a seat between the bird-like woman and the Sage. His old feelings of inadequacy and insecurity had returned in earnest. He sat in the presence of immense power; that much was clear. But the woman's insight into his heritage—a heritage he had only discovered the week prior—disturbed him. How could she have known?

Amarice told the shamans of the dreams she and Quinn had shared. Since there were no records of dream magic among the Scholar's histories, and they now knew Quinn had Deyoni blood, she asked them if they had any guidance for them. The old man nodded. "You are the resolution." He said no more.

Quinn and Amarice waited for a more helpful answer. The shamans did not speak. The air around them felt weighted, as if a pressure threatened to crush them under the force of the magic concentrated in this circle. Amarice enveloped her and Quinn in a protective air of peace before addressing the Deyoni again. "Please, *drabanas*, we don't understand."

The second woman spoke for the first time. "Shared dreams mean you are involved in the story. You are not outsiders in this darkness." She smoothed her skirts with her wrinkled hands.

"I do not know anything about Deyoni dream magic." Amarice's voice sounded desperate.

"Not Deyoni," the oldest woman spoke again. "*Tovari.*" She explained herself in the Deyoni language, unable to find the words in the common tongue. Amarice nodded, no emotion on her face. Quinn fought the urge to reach out and grab her hand to comfort her.

Amarice tried to explained to Quinn. "*Tovari* means half-blood. *Tovari* who are half-Scholar are the only ones who have dream magic. A 'melding of power,' she called it."

"Can we find another *Tovari* to explain this?"

Amarice shook her head. "We are probably the only ones alive right now. Few people mate with Deyoni, and Scholar's blood is even rarer."

No one said anything else. After some time, the shamans stood in one swift movement. Their meeting was done.

Quinn followed behind the Sage and the shamans slowly. He was just an apprentice who had only recently learned to control his earth magic. Now, he had learned he was somehow part of the resolution of this darkness spreading through Elandria, threatening his people.

The Deyoni did not stay the night. Walls, no matter how many windows and doors there were, were restrictive. Before they left, Quinn gathered the courage to ask more of the bird-like shaman. "Mother," he used the Deyoni address. The woman turned toward him. "I don't understand why I am the one having these dreams, why I'm the one involved. Is there some deeper reason, like a—a prophecy or something?"

The woman laughed harshly. "You are Scholar. There is no such thing as prophecies; you know this." She noticed Quinn's face filled with fear and confusion and softened her voice. "If every person who had a dream come true was part of prophecy, most people would be part of prophecy." She smiled for the first time since her arrival. "I will try to find your father." Then she walked away and followed the other shamans out of the Villa and down the mountain.

"Well, Brigitte's tit, that was incredibly unsatisfying," Quinn said aloud. Amarice agreed.

THE SAGE'S SABBATH dawned rainy and humid. Quinn was surprised to find, considering he lived with the Sage herself, that the holiday was not nearly as heavily celebrated as the Feast of Fire. The day that marked the beginning of spring and honored the birthday of the first Sage, Brigitte, passed without event.

Amarice pushed aside her dark mood that had come after meeting with the shamans for the day and became her effervescent self. After a large luncheon, she led everyone in the gardens to plant the first of the spring crops, a Sage's Sabbath tradition. Everyone laughed in a light-hearted spirit as they knelt in the mud and planted their seeds. The Scholars in the group kept the rain from falling on everyone's heads with their magic. Quinn was pleased he could now keep himself dry in rainy weather.

Once everyone changed out of their muddy clothes, they retired to play parlor games and sing folk songs. That was it. There were no traditional festival games (Quinn blamed the weather), no pouring of libations in honor of Brigitte, and no stories of the ancient war where Brigitte led the people of Elandria to victory.

The evening wound down, and many Villa residents went off to celebrate the Sage's Sabbath in the Teleah fashion—in their bedrooms with a lover. Quinn stoked the fire with his magic and moved to sit on a chair near Amarice. She smiled at him. "Winter is over," she said. "May the spring bring a new peace." Quinn nodded and raised his glass of mead to her.

"I have to say, this was the most toned down Sage's Sabbath I've ever celebrated," Quinn remarked. Amarice's smiled faded, and she shifted in her seat. "Is it because of recent events?"

Amarice stared through Quinn for a few moments before shaking her head no. "We do normally play some games outside, but the rain..." Her voice trailed. She sighed. "I don't think much of Brigitte, personally. She used her Gift of the Earth not for aid, not for self-defense, but to massacre the Deyoni who had resided in the Valley for thousands of years."

"But she felt guilty and tried to make amends," Quinn said, not to challenge Amarice, but to help himself cling to the idea that Scholars were always good people.

Amarice shrugged. "Did she try enough? I guess we weren't there to know. But I think the earth removed much of the power it gives because of her actions, so no one has had her power."

"Until you," Quinn observed.

Amarice gave him a sad smile. "It can be quite lonely." She stood, ending the conversation abruptly, and retired to her chambers, leaving Quinn alone with his mead in the parlor. Quinn knew the feeling of loneliness well; his heart ached for Amarice. Someone like her does not deserve the pain of being alone.

⚜

DROWNING. Suffocating. Falling. The darkness enveloped Quinn, and he felt every frightening sensation one could feel. He cried out, and no help came. He cried out again, his fear threatening to rip out of his chest and attack. He screamed as loud as he could; his magic spiraled out of control. Through the darkness, he felt the earth shake. He was vaguely aware of trees falling. Others screamed in fear.

And then a sharp pain pierced his chest. He could no longer scream; warm liquid filled his throat. He saw blood, red, thick, dripping. The darkness became painted in the warm crimson of his own blood. The magic stopped.

He stopped.

⚜

QUINN'S HEART POUNDED. He clutched his chest where the sharp pain had been. He feared to open his eyes, but he forced himself. His eyes grew accustomed the moonlit room, and he was safe in his bed. There was no blood. Finding his breath, Quinn felt compelled to take a walk. He needed to calm his racing heart and find his center in the earth. He left his room, barefoot to ground himself, and walked quietly through the Villa.

Wandering with no direction in mind, he found himself in the garden on the northern side of the Villa. The garden was already occupied. Past the roses, a figure he knew too well stared off into the Sage Mountains.

"Amarice?"

The Sage turned toward him. "You, too?" Quinn nodded and approached her. "What did you see?" She turned back toward the horizon. Her opalescent nightgown flapped gently in the midnight breeze. Her back and shoulders were bare, and she shivered.

"Darkness. Suffocating darkness like before. But this time I saw red, splattered like..." His voice drifted off. He didn't want to give voice to what he suspected.

"Blood."

"Yes." Quinn drew nearer to her, barely a hand's space away. They stood quietly for some time, grounding themselves in the cool, moist earth, calming their thoughts, reconnecting with their magic. Quinn's heartbeats slowed, and he once again felt like himself. Though shaken, his mind was clear, and his practical nature began to return. He broke the long silence. "What does it mean?"

Amarice turned to face him. In the moonlight, he could see her eyes were red and tears were streaming from her face. He had never seen her cry; he suspected few people had. Despite everything, he believed she had never looked more beautiful. He could feel the pain in her soul and ached to comfort her. Without thinking, he lifted a hand and gently wiped her tears.

"Quinn," she breathed. For a moment, she resisted.

In the next moment, neither of them sure how it happened, their lips met. Quinn kissed her feverishly, and she met him with equal force. Months of pent-up desire coupled with their shared fear and uncertainty went into the kiss. Quinn's left hand ran down her bare spine and rested at the small of her back, pulling her closer. He intertwined his other hand in her soft hair. She embraced him. The kiss took on a magic of its own; nothing had ever felt so right for either of them. For a brief eternity, there was no darkness.

When they parted, the Sage trembled. She had taken many lovers in her life, but nothing had ever felt like Quinn's kiss. She forced her breath to calm itself and took one step back. Quinn reached toward her, but she shook her head. Tears fell from her eyes again. "We can't," she whispered.

"I love you," he replied, confused. Had she not felt what he did when they kissed?

She did not reply right away. She chewed her lip, thinking. After several minutes, she spoke. "The world is too uncertain. A darkness threatens our magic, our world. I am the Sage; my very essence is rooted in earth magic. And you will not be my apprentice forever."

Quinn did not know how to respond. He knew she loved him, too. He felt it in her kiss. What was she not saying?

Amarice stared off into the night, the beacon of Elandria's hope faltering under the weight of her fear. Fear of the threat to Scholars and Deyoni alike. Fear of what darkness lie on her path. Fear of falling in love, and fear of a broken heart. She did not want to hurt Quinn, but she could not open herself to a man who would leave her in a few months' time. She would rather hurt his feelings now than later. Or worse, make him feel obligated to stay and not pursue his own dreams. She loved him too much to do that.

CHAPTER 15

"My lady, I think I should return to the Academy."

The Sage glanced up from her correspondence to see Quinn pacing in the study. She raised an eyebrow, signaling him to continue. He did not; he only continued to pace, wringing his hands. She watched him for a few moments. "Sit down. You're making me nervous pacing like that." He sat perched on the edge of the leather sofa as if he expected to bolt out of here at any moment.

A few days had passed since their kiss. Though not unfriendly, Amarice had become much more formal in addressing Quinn. She suspected that is what prompted him to address her as "my lady." Quinn had reverted to his shy, insecure self. They had interacted little; Quinn had stayed out of her way while he worked on pro-Deyoni literature.

Amarice eyed her apprentice. "Are you saying you don't want to complete your apprenticeship?"

Quinn rubbed his head with his hand. "I don't know." He said nothing else. Amarice used her Gift to create a space of safety, hoping he would feel comfortable enough to talk. They did need to talk, after all. Quinn felt an instant weight lifted off him. He knew he needed to tell her how he felt. "I'm not sure I can stay this close to you."

Her heart ached. She wished she could tell him she loved him in return, but she needed to protect herself. With the encroaching threat to Elandria—they still did not know what their latest dream meant— she was also protecting him. At least, that is what she kept telling herself. But she was determined to fall out of love with him so that she would not be left alone when his apprenticeship ended. If he was determined to have a career in diplomacy, he would need to return to Teleah. Of course, she had considered taking him as a lover that she met on occasion, like Raymond. But with Quinn—no, it simply would not work. It was better to never cave in to her desire.

But she did not want him to leave yet—for his sake. Completing an apprenticeship with the Sage would ensure he had countless career options at the end of the year. And there was still the fact that he shared these dreams of darkness with her. The Deyoni shamans seemed confident the resolution involved him. She looked at the handsome man sitting in front of her, hurt and inhibition plastered across his face.

"Quinn." She kept her voice as steady as she could. "I won't force you to stay, but I think you should continue your apprenticeship. It will be good for your future." She paused, replaying the most recent nightmare in her head. "And the dreams..."

Quinn nodded, trying hard to keep his face stoic. "It was the worst yet. But, after, in the garden..." His voice trailed off, too.

Amarice felt her lip quiver, and bit it to stop. How he wished she would not bite her lip! For a moment, he had thought she was right. But there she sat, exquisite in her sadness, and he wanted to once again run away back to Teleah to save his heart. If she would just tell him to stay, he would. He would do anything for her. But she would never tell him to do something he did not want.

"Give yourself some time before you decide, please. Don't make a hasty decision." She gave him one last sad gaze and lowered her head back to the letters in front of her. Quinn stood to leave. She was right, as usual. He would give himself a week to decide, to see if he could bear being in her presence with his unrequited love. Until then, he would continue making the literature to disseminate.

He started to leave her study to return to his room, then stopped. "Amarice?" She looked up again. "Has there been any news about the last dream?"

She shook her head. "No, it concerns me that we have heard nothing. I'll let you know as soon as I do." He nodded and left her alone.

A WEEK PASSED with no news. Amarice had returned to her bright self with Quinn instead of the formal, businesslike persona she had adopted after their kiss. In many ways, this hurt Quinn so much more. At least her change in demeanor had made him think the kiss had meant something to her. Now, he was unsure.

He had to leave. He would go back to the Academy and complete his fifth year studying the Deyoni. There were enough tribes near Teleah that he could gain firsthand knowledge. Although, without Amarice's guidance and translation, he wondered if they would accept him. Maybe he could find the bird-like shaman again. He made a mental note to ask Amarice where he could find her.

The morning had dawned grey and cloudy. Quinn had missed breakfast to begin packing. He would tell Amarice this afternoon that he was leaving and depart in the morning. He dreaded saying goodbye to the others; he had grown to love the Villa family as his own, and he did not want to admit he had failed in his apprenticeship because he could not put aside his feelings for Amarice.

He lined the bottom of his trunk with his books, then began folding his clothes from the wardrobe. He thought of his trip to the palace as he removed the black silk shirt from the shelf. He smiled at the memory, when he heard a voice behind him. "Quinn."

He turned. Amarice stood in the open doorway, her face streaked with tears. Her hands shook; she held a letter. She had news, and he sensed it was the worst yet. He looked at her, fear spreading throughout his body. She spoke again, her voice a sob. "Oh, Quinn."

"What is the news?" His voice quavered.

She swallowed audibly. Fresh tears fell from her red eyes. "It's Rafe."

In that instant, Quinn's whole world crumbled. He felt the floor fall out beneath his feet. He fell to his knees. "NO!" his voice cracked, but no tears fell. It was not disbelief he felt; he knew in his heart it was true. The weight of the grief was nearly too much to bear. "Tell me," he managed to say in a whisper. He did not meet her eyes.

Amarice cleared her throat, desperate to retain composure for Quinn's sake. But she felt his grief as if it were her own. "Viridion's students, all five of them. They were attacked at the Forest of Seluya." She said no more. She wanted to spare him the details of his friend's grisly murder.

"How?"

"Quinn, you don't want to—"

"HOW?" he yelled.

She clenched her eyes closed. He deserved to know. He was more involved in this tragedy than her now. Still, she wanted to save him the pain. "They—they were attacked. One, a girl named Melina, was hanged and mutilated like the last." She had to stop. It was so much harder to say than to read it from the letter. "The others were supposed to be, it seems. But, their combined fear caused wild magic. Many trees uprooted, and the campfire began to burn out of control. So, the rest... Rafe... they were stabbed through the heart."

Quinn stared at the floor. Amarice did not know what to do. She wanted to comfort him, but she did not know if that is what he needed. She knelt to be at his level, waiting for some response. He spoke after a few minutes. "He had to watch her die?" He looked up at Amarice, who simply nodded. "I'll kill whoever did this." His voice was flat. Amarice nodded again.

He stood, slowly. "I need to—excuse me." He pushed past her and began to run. He ran through the courtyard and out into the gardens. He kept running to the river. He ran along the banks, pushing himself harder until his breathing ached, and kept going. He ran until his side ached and kept going. The physical pain was a relief from the emotions that threatened to overtake him. He ran, ignoring the cold splashes of water from the river, the rocks and twigs that dug into his feet.

It must have been hours before he stopped. He only stopped when he physically could run no more. His legs throbbed, and his chest ached from the lack of air. He panted and took in his surroundings.

He had never been this far into the Sage's Mountains. He felt dwarfed by the green peaks. He found himself at the edge of some woods. The trees brought back the grief in a tidal wave. Rafe had died, protecting trees, protecting the earth that gave him life. Quinn fell to the ground and screamed. Birds squawked and flew off in droves at the noise. He screamed until his voice left him and his throat ached. It's nothing compared to his pain, he thought bitterly.

Anger flowed through his body like fire. He would find whoever did this, whoever was behind this. And he would make sure they hurt the way they had hurt his best friend.

CHAPTER 16

The Academy for Scholars held a funeral for the five murdered students the following week. It was lovely and respectful, held outdoors like the annual commencement ceremony these students would never have. In contrast to the overwhelming grief, the warm spring sun shone brightly in a cloudless blue sky. The stage and the end of every row of seats had been decorated with vibrant chrysanthemums of mourning—out of season, but grown with the purest of earth magic.

Amarice sat as Sage with the professors and the king on the stage. She had declined to speak words of comfort during the funeral; her heart ached too badly to assume her role of their leader. Quinn had been withdrawn and addled since receiving the news, often forgetting what he was saying mid-sentence. He had unpacked his trunk, though. Amarice searched the crowd for him. She tried to avoid looking at the distraught families in the front rows; it would be hard enough to shake their hands later in condolence. At this moment, she loathed her role as Sage. She longed to be sitting with Quinn to comfort him.

Her eyes settled on him several rows back, next to a redheaded young man she assumed was Jack. Quinn wore his black ensemble again, in contrast to the reds and oranges that were customary for funerals. She imagined it fit his mood well. He was angry and frightened. He had bottled his grief deep inside him, and she knew it threatened to overtake him. She could just make out that his face was stony, emotionless. Beside him, Jack's face had a combined look of sadness and shock.

A few students played a funerary song on their pipes and stringed-instruments, while a young female sang. Her voice was chilling, and many in the crowd began to sob loudly, unable to hold back the emotions. The mother of the girl who had "SIN" carved on her chest screamed in agony. Quinn still sat stone-faced, unable even to comfort Jack, who had been overcome by violent, shaking sobs.

Professor Viridion, who had been the students' mentor, began reading a eulogy he had prepared. He could not finish. His high voice broke, and he began to weep inconsolably. "I'm so sorry," he repeated over and over, until the other professors managed to pull him away from the podium. Professor Quickthorn took over the eulogy, reading the words Viridion had prepared with a sort of removed tone. Viridion's cries tore at Amarice's heart, and she enveloped herself in a bubble of peace.

After the eulogy, the king addressed the grieving crowd. "We will find who is behind this, and they will suffer the wrath of the Elandrian people," he promised. He spoke with a kingly confidence, though Amarice knew he had few leads. Warnings of evil continued to be preached in the small villages, but no one confessed to any action.

Quickthorn tapped Amarice on the shoulder. "You're up, my Lady Sage." Amarice nodded, and met Quinn's eyes through the crowd before she stood. His held no light.

The Sage descended the steps of the stage, grabbing five chrysanthemums from a vase at the edge. She walked toward the small pile of wood in the front of the stage. She sighed. It was customary for the Sage to draw the fire if she was present at the funeral. Amarice was aware that every eye was on her, and she hated it. This was not about her; any Scholar here could have started the fire. Wordlessly, she used her magic to light the flames as quickly as she could.

The fire roared to life. It was a small blaze, but it crackled and burned. The heat could be felt at least five rows back. She named each of the murdered students, one by one, and tossed in a chrysanthemum for each. When she got to the fifth name, her voice cracked. "Rafe Reardan." She held out the last flower, a deep scarlet, and dropped in into the flames. She let it incinerate completely before she turned away and went back to the stage.

The crowds began to rise from their seats and made their way to the fire. Some said only the name of their lost loved one. Others threw in five flowers because they had known them all. Amarice waited for last of the funeral guests to throw in their flowers and disperse before descending the stage again to offer her condolences to the families.

Quinn and Jack were two of the last to throw their chrysanthemums in the fire. They spoke the name of their beloved friend together and watched the flowers burn. Jack put his arm around Quinn, seeking the comfort of his living friend. Quinn did not have it in him to oblige.

After a few moments, Jack spoke. "Come on, Quinn. We need to see his mother." He was right, but Quinn dreaded it. Rafe had been close to his mother, and he knew the woman must be barely keeping herself together. He had never met her, but she was easy to spot. She had Rafe's green eyes and black hair, though hers was touched with grey. A teen girl stood next to her; she must have been Rafe's beloved little sister. They were both talking to the Sage.

"He always wanted to meet you," Rafe's mother told the Sage as Quinn and Jack approached.

Amarice forced a sad smile. "I wanted to meet him, too. My apprentice loved him dearly." Quinn swallowed at those words. Amarice looked up and saw him standing there; she was fully in her role as Sage, but her grey eyes held the grief one feels for a dear friend who is hurting. It was too hard to look at her face. Instead, he focused on the diadem resting on her hair, trying to separate himself from the flood of emotions.

Rafe's mother turned to see Quinn and Jack standing awkwardly. They were unsure what to say. She broke into tears again and embraced them. This time, Quinn returned the hug. "He loved you both," she sobbed. "Thank you for being such great friends to him." She held them tight; Quinn could feel her tears wetting his shirt. He thought for a moment it was blood and felt a sharp pain over his heart. He tensed himself and forced it to go away.

After several minutes, she let them go. Quinn and Jack hugged Rafe's sister and murmured words of condolence. There were no words adequate to the situation. Finally, Rafe's family began to leave. His mother turned toward the young men one last time, but her eyes met Quinn's. "You were family to him; therefore, you are family to me. Please, do not be strangers." She turned and walked away, holding her daughter's hand.

Amarice spoke again. "Jack, I'm glad to meet you, although I wish it were under happier circumstances. Quinn has spoken highly of you. I'm so sorry for your loss." Jack forced a smile, but then tears fell from his eyes again. Quinn stood stoically. Amarice embraced Jack.

"Thank you." Jack pulled away. He gave a wet laugh. "Never thought I'd hug the Sage of Elandria." He wiped his eyes. "Quinn, a few of us—we're going to Bucky's to drink to Rafe."

Quinn shook his head. "I can't." Jack nodded.

"Well, be safe. See you soon." He embraced Quinn, and this time, Quinn clung to him tight. He did not want to lose Jack, too.

⚜

THE CARRIAGE RIDE BACK to the palace was silent. He shared the carriage with Amarice, and she did not make him talk. He was glad; just being in her presence was enough. They ate a quick dinner with the king; Raymond was not in Teleah. Thankfully, the king did not wish to discuss the attacks. He sensed the funeral had taken its toll on both the Sage and her young apprentice. What conversation they held was empty and meaningless.

Both Quinn and Amarice retired early to their rooms. He undressed, putting on only a pair of light linen pants in which to sleep. He was exhausted from grief, but he could not even doze. He thought of all the things he had never said to Rafe. He never told him how much he appreciated his friendship, how he loved him like a brother. He remembered his last promise to Rafe. His patient friend never pushed Quinn to talk about his life, but he genuinely cared. One day,

I'll tell you all about me. He should have told him then, or any time over the last four and a half years. He should have been a better friend.

Hours passed as Quinn sat thinking, alone in the palace bedroom. He did not even notice the sunset. He sat in the darkness. He felt numb, and frightened, and angry, and lonely. He suddenly became vastly aware of his loneliness. He thought it would suffocate him.

He thought of Amarice. She had looked so lovely in her red silk dress today. She was the only light in this otherwise dark day. He felt a rush of desire fight against the grief in his heart. His heart ached, and part of it was aching for her.

Before he could overthink it, he left his room and knocked on the door next to his. Amarice opened the door. She wore her shiny white nightgown that gathered behind her neck again. Her brown hair fell unpinned over her bare shoulders. She was not wearing her Scholar's pendant or her Sage's diadem. In this moment, she was purely Amarice.

"Quinn?" She sounded surprised to see him. He did not respond, but stepped toward her. He leaned his head down and kissed her. She parted her lips, inviting in his tongue. She shivered as he ran his hands over the soft skin of her back.

She was no longer thinking. She threw her arms around his neck and stood as high as she could to kiss him. He lifted her in response, and she wrapped her legs around his waist. She could feel him growing hard beneath his pants. He kicked the door closed with one foot and carried Amarice to the bed, where laid her down gently.

He stroked her hair with one hand as he kissed her. She placed her hand on his bare chest, over his pounding heart. With his other hand, he unhooked her dress and exposed her voluptuous breasts. He caressed them as he lowered his kisses to her chin, her neck, and lower. She moaned and moved her hand down his chiseled chest to the trail of hair that led into his pants. She was overcome by desire.

But as he began to pull off the rest of her dress, she became conscious of the situation. "No," she murmured. "Quinn, no. Not like this." He pulled his hand away, looking confused. Oh, he looked good when he was confused. She shook herself. "Quinn, you're hurting. We can't."

He looked her in her eyes. "Don't you want..." His voice trailed.

"Yes, oh so much. But," she paused. "You're only doing this now because you need to let yourself feel something." He continued gazing at her face. "This isn't the way, Quinn. Just let yourself grieve."

Quinn held her gaze for a moment longer. And then he burst into tears. He did not remember the last time he had cried. Maybe he shed a few tears when he left Corthy. He could not recall. But tonight, the tears fell in earnest. First, it was just the tears. Then he fell into sobs so strong he could barely breathe. He cried for Rafe. And when he had no tears left for Rafe, he cried for not knowing his real father. He cried for the way he had shamed his family, for the way his village had treated him. He cried because he missed his brother. He cried because he was deeply in love with the woman next to him. And he cried for all the darkness that had crept into his country and all the people who had been lost.

Amarice fastened her gown back then held him in her arms. She offered no words of comfort, just her embrace. He sobbed for hours, and she held him the entire time. She ran her fingers through his brown hair, for once not parted carefully.

His sobs turned into tearful gasps after several hours. He yawned. "Go to sleep," she murmured in his ear. "I'm right here." He gave one last sob before his eyes closed and his breathing slowed. She pulled the blanket over him and laid her head on her own pillow before falling into a dreamless slumber.

◌◌◌

QUINN AWOKE THE NEXT MORNING, disoriented and eyes glued shut from crying the night before. His arm was wrapped around something. Someone? Oh, no. He peeled open his eyes. Amarice lay beneath his arm, sleeping peacefully. She looked beautiful, he noticed, with no weight of responsibility on her face.

But he could not keep holding her. He wondered how long they had slept like this. He removed his arm and shifted, trying to find the clock. He squinted at the hands on the large clock face across from the bed. Nine-thirty. He could not remember the last time he had slept so late.

Amarice moaned and twisted in the bed. Unsure what to do, Quinn laid back down. He could wake her, although she had stayed up late comforting him while he cried. She probably needed the sleep. He could sneak back to his room. But would that be rude? They had slept together, but they had not slept together. Still, they had shared an intensely emotional night. And they had almost...

His mind wandered back to the beginning of their night. He thought of her breasts, her lips, her touch. She was right to stop, he knew, but if she had just stopped a bit later. He forced himself to think about something else.

He took an internal inventory of his emotions, as Amarice had coached him over the last several months. Though his heart still ached for Rafe, he felt better, lighter. Most importantly, he felt. I probably should not go years without crying, he thought. He laughed at himself.

Amarice stirred and opened her eyes. She, too, had a look of disorientation. But when she realized Quinn was there, she did not panic. Instead, she smiled sleepily. "Good morning," she yawned. Oh, she was exquisite, here in bed with no pretense. Quinn wished he had this view every morning. Stop, he told himself. She was the friend you needed last night.

He smiled in return. "Good morning."

Amarice sat up in bed and cracked her neck. "How do you feel?" she asked.

"Better. Thank you for..." For what? Listening to him cry? That sounded inadequate. She waved her hand as if it were no issue. "And about before that—I'm sorry. That was inappropriate."

She smiled, a touch of regret in her eyes. "Don't be sorry," she said, with a nonchalance she did not feel. She changed the subject. "What time is it?"

"Half-past nine."

Her eyes widened. "We should get ready to leave. My poor driver is probably waiting, very confused." She crossed the room to her satchel and pulled out a purple gauzy dress. She turned and looked at Quinn.

He mumbled a word of apology and left her room quickly to get dressed.

The carriage ride back to the Villa was amicable and, to Quinn's surprise, not awkward. They spoke casually, and Quinn even shared some of his favorite stories of Rafe. He loved hearing her laughter ring through the enclosed carriage.

They arrived at the Villa in time for dinner. All the residents offered their condolences to Quinn, and he could accept them with gratitude. Amarice excused herself to go to bed early, citing emotional exhaustion. Before she retired, she told Quinn, "You're not done grieving, and that is fine. Take the time you need." He nodded and smiled. Though he loved her, he could appreciate her as a friend and confidante if nothing more.

And he could still enjoy watching her leave the room, he thought to himself, as she walked away.

CHAPTER 17

The next few months passed without event. No further attacks occurred, but the king's Inquisitors had no new leads either. The Academy issued a call for all Scholars in rural villages to return to larger towns or the cities, where there was no anti-magic sentiment. Many chose to return to Teleah, as the Sage had predicted. The Villa became much busier, and Quinn found it harder and harder to find quiet time to work on his magic.

With the new residents, interpersonal relationships often suffered. A new lover's quarrel happened in the courtyard every other day, it seemed. Quinn had to politely turn down more than one young Scholar's offer to join their bed. Jack and Rafe would have killed him, he knew, but he was still grieving. The days got easier, but every so often, a wave of emotion would hit him like a punch in the gut. And, though their relationship had turned into a solid friendship, Quinn still only wanted one woman in his bed.

Amarice had been so impressed with Quinn's pro-Deyoni literature that she ordered it printed and disseminated in every city, town, and village in Elandria. He had carefully collected the facts that made the Deyoni relatable to the rest of Elandria's citizens and compiled it into exquisitely worded pamphlets and posters. Thus, the cities saw a decrease in tensions, and Amarice expressed her immense pride in her apprentice. Sentiments remained unchanged in the villages, the Inquisitors reported, but thankfully the Deyoni remained safe by staying near the protection of the cities.

Quinn had a confidence he had never felt before. He kept his magic, now stronger than most Scholars', well-controlled. Amarice continued to push him to new limits. He lived for his private lessons with her, when they would go to the valley north of the Villa to manip- ulate nature's forces to their will.

"Why do you always come to this spot?" he had finally asked her one day.

"Can't you feel it? The magic is strongest here. I have walked these mountains for years. This is the heart of the earth." She was right, of course, once he bothered to pay attention. He had felt great magic here, but had never compared it to the rest of the mountain. Now he could feel a distinct difference, and his morning runs usually brought him here to refill his well of power. And his new afternoon runs, which he used to escape from the noise and drama at the Villa.

He had succeeded in changing the speed of the river by now, and he played a crucial part in the spring's planting. He worked with the other Scholars to distill plant oils and improved his knowledge of healing.

Quinn asked Amarice to teach him the language of the Deyoni. He wanted to continue to learn about them and write about them, but he could only gather so much from the biased books he read. Lessons were slow, as Amarice had never taught anyone a language before. For the first time, he learned that she also spoke two other languages fluently, and she had been trying to teach herself Lazori. He had a feeling he could apprentice with her the rest of his life and still learn something new about this incredible woman every day.

"I like to read books in their original language," she told him. "There are good books out there from other lands." Quinn was unsure he had ever read a book that was not from Elandria. Their country had the worldwide reputation for being the land of knowledge and educa- tion, and most books that existed were Elandrian in origin. Amarice then loaded him up with a stack of her favorite translated foreign books.

He pored through them, and they discussed them over meals. They mostly kept to themselves, and he often noticed the Villa's residents, old and new, whispering and looking in his and the Sage's direction. Quinn did not care.

He made progress with his Deyoni, but they had no written language, so they struggled together. He asked her how she had learned. "I don't know. My mother spoke Deyoni most of the time, so I learned it when I learned our language."

They made a few more short trips to the capital for meetings with the Chief Inquisitor, although he had little to report. In town, Quinn made a point to see both Jack and Rafe's mother. It hurt to see her, but she welcomed Quinn as if he were family. She always fixed him a meal, and they shared happy memories of Rafe. Jack, on the other hand, was not well. Rafe's death had taken a much larger toll on him than Quinn had expected. He had lost weight, and his cheerful demeanor had become solemn. Quinn worried about him and wrote to him far more often than he had before.

Amarice's birthday fell at the beginning of summer. She requested a small to-do, although nothing held at the Villa was small anymore. But the original Villa family settled in for dessert, drinks, and gifts after dinner. She opened Quinn's gift, and a grin spread across her face.

He had bought her a brightly colored, woven Deyoni rug in shades of purple and green. "I'm still sorry about your other rug," he said with a sheepish grin.

"Try not to burn this one up. I love it. It's gorgeous."

"I spoke in Deyoni to buy it, too. Well, I tried, at least. I think I damn near bought you a sheep, but pointing is the universal language." Everyone laughed, imagining shy Quinn using broken Deyoni to barter with the seller.

❦

ONE RETURN TRIP FROM TELEAH, they stopped in the Deyoni camps again. They were once more treated with a show, this time including fire-eaters and acrobatics. Quinn was amazed at their talent; indeed, he found them a bit frightening. He wondered if he would have been taught to eat fire or perform elaborate leaps in the air had he been raised by his father. His father, who he had not seen again.

Quinn stumbled over his limited Deyoni, which delighted all of them. Some of the children taught him swear words, lying about their meaning. Amarice watched and laughed, making a note to correct him later.

He was quiet on the rest of the carriage ride. "Were you hoping to see your father?"

"I just want to talk to him, to know his name. I feel like I've almost figured out this piece of myself that was missing for so long, but it's just out of reach." But he knew it was unlikely; there were now close to ten thousand Deyoni outside of the city. He wondered if the shaman was looking for him, too, or if her words had been an empty promise.

Amarice reached out and squeezed his hand. "I'm sorry," she told him. He smiled. Her words were genuine; everything about Amarice was. Amarice could not make an empty promise if she wanted—it just was not in her nature.

He changed the subject. "The Deyoni love you." She smiled. "Amarice, do you know if your mother is near Teleah with the others?"

Her smile faded. "She died a few years ago. She never returned to the tribes; she stayed in the village with my father's mother to care for her. But she passed first." Amarice bit her lip to suppress her tears. "I can't help but wonder if she would have lived longer if she had returned to the tribes. They move so often they rarely fall ill." This time, Quinn reached for her hand and squeezed it.

"I wish I could have met her."

"I wish I could have met Rafe," she replied. They smiled sadly at each other and continued the journey in silence.

CHAPTER 18

Quinn could hardly believe his luck. He had been Amarice's apprentice for nearly seven months, and he had visited the palace several times. This time, however, he was preparing to attend the king's birthday celebrations. It was the biggest party of the year. Celebrations extended throughout the capital, and he had regularly gone out with his friends to enjoy the festivities. But now, he was on his way to celebrate with the king himself.

The Sage's carriage pulled over the bridge to the palace, and Amarice placed her diadem on her head. He watched her posture shift as she transformed into her formal role, no less beautiful but even more staggering in her power. The carriage stopped far before the palace gates. Quinn peered out the window.

"There's a long line of carriages," he told Amarice.

She shrugged. "The palace will be full tonight. Roland throws quite the party." She smoothed her dress. "Make your face known. Every minister and member of Parliament will be here. Introduce yourself as my apprentice if I am not around." She paused, not meeting his eyes. "Your apprenticeship will be over in a few months. We will need to start thinking about your career."

Quinn thought he heard a slight sadness in her voice, but he decided he must have imagined it. He found himself feeling much like he did last year: he had no clue what to do in the next stage of his life. He loved his research on the Deyoni, and he knew he could give an additional voice to them in politics. But he could not bear to think about leaving the Villa, about leaving Amarice. Perhaps she would let him stay as a permanent resident. Or perhaps it would be better if he just left and tried to move past her.

But he was not going to dwell on it tonight. The king's birthday had a reputation for being not only an excellent event to meet diplomats but also wildly entertaining. He wished he could celebrate with Jack and Rafe and wistfully remembered the last time he had gone out with them. Rafe had been dancing and singing on tables when Quinn had gone upstairs with Sarah. He smiled to himself.

"What are you smiling about?" Amarice asked in a warm voice.

"Just thinking how much Rafe would have enjoyed a party at the palace," he said. Amarice reached out and patted his knee.

"Have a few drinks in his honor, then."

The carriage finally pulled in front of the gates, and a lanky butler opened the carriage door. "My lady Sage, welcome back." He drew his hand to his brow in greeting. "Mr. Atwell, welcome to you, as well." Amarice took the butler's hand and stepped out of the carriage. Quinn followed, and two other servants rushed forward to collect their belongings.

Quinn squinted in the bright sun gleaming off the white palace walls. Extra banners with the royal family's sigil—a blue bear on a gold background—had been hung, along with yards upon yards of blue and gold ribbon that hung from every tree and doorway. Thousands of blue flowers lined the courtyard and shrubbery had been carved into the shape of bears. The whole palace emanated an aura of festivity.

The butler escorted Amarice and Quinn to their normal rooms, which now felt like "home away from home" to Quinn. As he dressed, he recalled the night he had knocked on Amarice's door. A part of him hoped he could wake beside her again in the morning. But he forced himself back into reality. They were good friends now, but no more. Besides, I'm sure Prince Raymond will find his way into her bed again. He shook off the envy and laced his leather breeches.

He pulled his new silk shirt over his head, a bright blue in honor of the king. He put on his Scholar's pendant and combed his hair, wondering what Amarice would be wearing tonight. She did look exquisite in blue. But she looked exquisite in everything. And nothing, he smiled to himself. Get a grip, Quinn. He smacked his face in reprimand and tried to push the image of Amarice in her bed out of his head.

A knock on his door made his heart leap. He crossed the room a little too quickly and flung open the door. He gasped in shock at the wonder standing in front of him. "Oh, my lady Sage," he murmured, because in this instant she deserved to be worshipped.

Amarice looked ethereal. A layer of thin sapphire tulle stretched over her bosom and opened over a sheath of silk in shades of lavender and violet. Her sleeves began in the middle of her arm, leaving her soft shoulders bare, and draped to the floor like purple and blue wings. An elaborate belt of thin gold decorated with sapphire teardrops accentuated her waist. Her beauty was nothing short of mythical.

She grinned and twirled around so he could see the back of her dress. The sapphire fabric fit loosely under the gold belt. Half of her thick, brown hair cascaded over her back, the rest lay braided around her diadem. "Do you like it?" she asked. "It's new."

"You look like a dream. A very good dream."

She grinned. "Can you help me with my necklace?" She held up a gold choker lined with sapphire gems that matched her belt. Quinn swallowed and nodded. She turned her back to him again and swept up her hair into her hands. She smelled of roses and honey, and Quinn's brain grew foggy.

He placed the necklace around her neck and slowly fastened it, breathing in her scent. He could not help himself and ran one hand over her bare shoulder. She shivered. He touched his lips to her shoulder softly. "Quinn," she breathed and turned to face him. She gazed up into his big brown eyes, her breaths heavy.

"All finished," he whispered. She said nothing, but her eyes danced with conflicted desire. Another door down the hall opened, forcing them both back to reality. Words hung unspoken in the air between them.

"Well. Let's go." She turned to walk toward the party, and Quinn followed her down the stairs without a word. As they approached the large ballroom, a line began to form. An attendant was calling out the name of each guest as they entered. The line moved quickly as ministers and foreign visitors and merchants were announced. "Take my arm," she whispered as they drew close to the door.

"What?"

"Take my arm. We have to enter together since you are my apprentice." She held out her arm, and he took it cautiously in his. They were next. The attendant looked at them and smiled. He knew their names.

"The Sage of Elandria, Amarice Teyvana, and her apprentice Quinn Atwell!" the man announced. Quinn took a deep breath. A round of applause sounded for the Sage. She led him down the marble steps into the ballroom.

Quinn had never seen such a lavish place in his life. The floors were marbled in black and white, and the walls, lined with silk banners of blue and gold, had to be at least twenty feet high. Massive gold and diamond chandeliers hung from the ornately carved ceilings. The guests themselves added to the opulence, all dressed in their vibrant finery. Without a doubt, though, the most alluring guest was on his arm.

The Sage parted from him as they reached the bottom step and the attendant called the next name. He followed her into the crowd where she was immediately greeted by multiple people eager to make her acquaintance. She tried at first to introduce Quinn to everyone she met, but the crowds eventually pushed them apart. Quinn tried to avoid the suffocating hordes by moving the edge of the room.

He found himself next to the grand buffet, filled with more food than he had ever seen in his life. Mounds of meat lay on silver platters next to huge bowls of heaping vegetables and fruits and trays of warm breads. At the end of the table, the pastries lay like delicious works of art. Quinn's stomach growled at the aromas emanating from the feast.

"Quinn!" He turned to the sound of a familiar voice calling his name. A few feet away, a handsome redhead dressed in fine jade silks and brown leather breeches, pushed through the crowd to greet Quinn.

"Jack! What on earth are you doing here?" He greeted his friend with a warm hug and slap on the back.

"The old bastard is always invited," Jack replied, referring to the apothecary with whom he apprenticed. "But he hates anything fun, so he sent me to represent him." Jack had a glass of wine in his hand. "Let's get you a drink."

Quinn walked with him to the table where servants handed out wine and mead. The friends chatted, catching each other up on their lives. Jack seemed better, past much of his grief. Life was going well for him now. Many of Jack's regular customers had told him they would use his business over the old man's shop because of his talent and his far more pleasant demeanor. Jack had been looking for investors to help him after his apprenticeship ended and had several leads. Quinn mentioned how he was supposed to be meeting people who could give him work tonight, but many of the ministers were already several drinks deep.

Amarice made her way over after some time. Quinn gave her a longing smile, and she returned it with a demure glance. Jack gave Quinn a questioning look, but Quinn just smiled. Amarice greeted Jack as if they were old friends. Her beauty had even Quinn's confident friend stumbling over his words until he downed another glass of wine. She reminded Quinn to give his well-wishes to the king, then disappeared into the crowd again.

"What did that look mean, Quinn?" Jack asked curiously. "Are you and the Sage...?" He gestured obscenely.

"No. I don't know what you are talking about." Quinn took another glass of mead from the table, preferring it over the bitter red wine.

Jack gaped at him. "You're in love with her. And I think she's—"

"Drop it, please, Jack."

"No." He studied his empty glass. "Quinn, you need to know something. I was in love with Rafe."

Quinn was shocked, but said nothing. It explained how much harder Jack had taken Rafe's murder. He waited for his friend to continue.

"I never told him. He never liked men, so I figured it was a lost cause. But I loved him for years. And now, I regret not telling him. Even if we could not have been together, I wish he had known how I felt." Jack wiped a tear from his eye. "Don't waste an opportunity with the Sage."

Quinn's heart ached, for his friend and for his own love. Perhaps Jack was right. He would think on it later. Jack finally changed the subject.

They talked about how much Rafe would have enjoyed this, how much he had deserved a party at the palace. Jack updated Quinn on some of the latest gossip of their cohort, although Quinn found it far less reliable than Rafe's updates. Quinn looked over the heads of the crowd and noticed the king was no longer surrounded by a pack of people. He stood speaking only to Amarice and the prince.

The orchestra started playing a well-known court dance. A pretty blonde asked Jack to dance, and Quinn was once more left alone. After a moment, Amarice approached him again. "Do you know the dance?" she asked.

Quinn did, although he had not danced it since he had lived in Corthy. She pulled him on the dance floor, despite his protests. But she looked so happy, he would not let her down. He took her hands in his, and they danced in time to the upbeat song, skipping and turning with the other guests. Amarice locked eyes with him, and he could see only her.

The music changed to a waltz, and he placed a hand on her waist. She shivered, but followed his steps without a word. He spun her on the floor once, her dress twirling in blue and purple, and she met his eyes again. "Earlier, in the corridor..." Her voice trailed.

He thought back to his impulsive kiss of her shoulder. "I'm not going to apologize this time, Amarice." He spun her again.

"I don't want you to apologize. I want you—" She was interrupted by a tap on her shoulder. A parliament minister cut in; it would be rude for her to refuse. She gave Quinn an apologetic look as he left the dance floor. He wandered toward the back wall, watching her dance with other people. What was she going to say to him? He thought of

Jack's advice earlier; he would not let this conversation go. He would address it later, after the party.

The waltz ended, and Amarice and Jack found Quinn again. Amarice took a glass of mead from a servant Quinn had never seen before. Jack opted for wine.

Jack filled the conversation, and Amarice gave Quinn a smile that said she, too, wished to finish their dance floor conversation. After a few moments, though, she reminded Quinn he needed to give the king birthday wishes. "I'll introduce you, Jack," she promised. The two young men followed her to where the king and Prince stood.

They greeted the king, who seemed to be enjoying himself thoroughly. Quinn noticed Amarice stood several feet away from Raymond, and his heart took a little delight in it. She sipped her mead as the king inquired of Jack and his apprenticeship. Even he recognized Teleah's greatest apothecary was a bitter old man, and he made Jack laugh with some of his stories.

Quinn looked at Amarice. Her smile had been replaced by a look of, well, he was not sure. She did not look herself. "Are you well, my lady?" He used a formal address since there were various diplomats milling around.

She forced a smile. "I think I may have eaten something that did not agree with me. I will be fine." She tried her best to join in the conversation. Within several minutes, she had grown pale and sweaty. She kept forgetting her train of thought mid-sentence.

"Amarice?" Quinn's voice held a great deal of concern.

She gave him another weak smile. "I think I will retire for the evening. I have some tinctures in my room that are wonderful for nausea. Forgive me, King Roland. Happy Birthday." They assured her it was no trouble, and she walked toward the door. Quinn followed her, offering to escort her to her room. "I will be fine, Quinn. I just need some tea and to go to sleep. Stay. Enjoy the party." He nodded, but looked after her as she left, worried. He had never seen Amarice ill.

AMARICE'S MIND grew increasingly foggy. She shivered, cold, but was drenched in sweat. Her stomach churned. She felt as if she were walking through clouds. Somehow, she made her way up the stairs to the corridor where her guest room lay. The door seemed so far away.

Her legs grew heavy, and she willed herself to just get to the door. She could skip the tea and fall straight into bed. Her mind could barely focus, and her vision became blurred. Her last coherent thought was that she should have taken Quinn's offer of help to her room.

Then a sharp pain struck her head, and she fell to the hallway floor, unconscious.

⚜

QUINN RETURNED TO THE KING, the prince, and Jack, who had been joined by several other people Quinn did not know. He was pleased to see Jack easily rubbing elbows with Teleah's elite, but he could not enjoy himself. His thoughts kept returning to Amarice. After about fifteen minutes, he excused himself to go check on her.

As he climbed the stairs, a feeling of dread filled him. He entered the corridor cautiously, unsure why he felt wary. Halfway to her room, something shiny lay on the floor. His heart skipped a beat. He approached, and his whole world fell out from under him.

There lay her Sage's diadem, and a small pool of blood. "No," he gasped, disbelief and desperation mingling in his voice. "No." Unsure what to do, he pounded on her bedroom door. "AMARICE!" he yelled, but there was no answer, of course. He tried the doorknob; it was unlocked. She was gone, and it did not appear she had ever made it back from the party. Her dress from earlier lay in a pile on the floor, her satchel thrown carelessly on the bed. "Oh no," a sob caught in his throat. He took the diadem and ran back to the party.

"King Roland!" He rushed over to the king, interrupting his conversation. The king looked up at him, taken aback by his lack of decorum. Quinn held out the diadem, dripping blood onto the marble floor. "She's gone."

The king's eyes grew wide, and the guests surrounding him gasped in panic. Raymond signaled to one of the few guards; security was more of a formality in Elandria. "Lock down the palace. No one leaves.

Find the Sage." The king gave instruction to send the Chief Inquisitor to his study, then beckoned for Quinn and Raymond to follow him. Quinn followed, his hands shaking, still holding the bloody diadem. If only I had insisted on escorting her, he thought. He felt guilty and powerless. He wanted to run and find her, to question every one. But he maintained enough composure to know they needed to conduct a systematic search.

The king sat silently behind his desk. Raymond paced the study up and down, swearing at no one. Quinn sat on the sofa because he could do nothing else. The only light in the study was the fireplace and the moonlight through the window. No one bothered to light the lamps.

The Chief Inquisitor, Marcus, brought regular updates. It was clear she was not in the palace. No more blood hand been found. Hours passed. A stableman had been found unconscious near the carriages. Another hour passed. The palace Healer had roused the man. Four men, one dressed as a servant that he had never seen before, had placed the unconscious Sage in a nondescript wagon with a black horse before hitting him upside the head. Two hours passed. The Inquisitors found the city's gate guards that had been on watch. The southern gate guard was the only who had seen a wagon with a black horse.

"We have to go now, Father!" Raymond exclaimed. "They are already hours away." Quinn nodded vehemently in agreement.

"We don't know which way they went. They may have headed south, but they may be off the road. They may have veered to the east or west to throw us off their trail." The king placed his head in his hands. "We'll send out soldiers to question anyone who might have seen anything, and once we know more, we will send a search party."

Raymond swore violently. Quinn felt the urge to hit something. But the king was right. If they headed out in the wrong direction, they would lose even more valuable time to find Amarice. For now, there was nothing to do but wait.

CHAPTER 19

Amarice woke but did not open her eyes. Her head pounded in pain. She took a quick inventory of herself and her surroundings. She was quite sure she was bleeding from multiple parts of her body. She listened; she was moving and she could only hear the hooves of one horse. She thought it was light outside, but refrained from opening her eyes to make sure. She stifled a groan of pain.

As her senses came back to her, she made out the voices of men. It took some time to be certain, but she counted four men's voices. She tried to stay still, to make them think she still slept. That was not hard; her head felt as if it had been split in two. She forced herself to listen to their conversation.

One kicked her in the gut. "How much did you slip in her drink, Blake? Shouldn't she be awake by now?" His voice was gruff.

Another man responded. "Two drops." Blake, she thought. Now if I can get the others to say their names.

A third man spoke. "Better she's out. Don't want her castin' spells on us. Shoulda gagged her. Too late now. She might wake up. Idiots." The men bickered a bit about who was actually an idiot. Then the conversation turned to how evil the Sage was; at least they all agreed on that much. The words "demon" and "sorcerer" featured heavily in the conversation, along with "bitch who doesn't know her place" and "Deyoni mutt." Amarice felt the situation declining by the minute. And damn, her head ached.

"How long till we get to Charles?" Blake asked.

The man who wanted to gag her responded. "If we rest the horse, then buy a new one in the village tomorra', it'll be three more days." He said nothing for a few minutes. "Can't wait to deliver her to answer for her sins."

"Think he'll do what we done to the last couple? Demon or not, I'd like to see this one stripped down before she's hung."

Amarice felt a wave of nausea that had nothing to do with the poison. "Lust not after demons though disguised as angels," the gruff man quoted. "That's what Charles says." Who the fuck is Charles? Amarice thought.

The fourth man spoke. "He'll make a much bigger example of this one. She's the worst of the lot, and she'll get the king's attention." He spat, and Amarice felt a large blob of saliva fall on her arm. She pushed aside the urge to gag.

The men said no more for some time. Amarice allowed herself to drift back into sleep. Her head ached, and she still felt groggy from whatever Blake had put in her drink. She also suspected she had lost a fair share of blood. She fell to sleep and dreamed a vast darkness lay between her and Quinn. It was a terrible dream, but she could see his face, which it made it far better than her current reality.

QUINN HAD NOT SLEPT all night. He was still in the king's study, sitting in the same position on the sofa. The king had dozed for a couple hours, snoring upright in his chair. Raymond had at least stopped pacing to lay on the sofa opposite Quinn, but he was unsure if the prince had slept.

A maid brought up a tray of pastries and fruit for breakfast. The king ate, but Raymond and Quinn declined the food. They only wanted one thing—to know where Amarice was. Just past eight o'clock, Marcus returned with an update.

"They definitely went south on the road for several miles before heading off road. My Inquisitors have spread out to question as many as they can. It's daylight. We'll find a witness. If they don't buy a second horse, they will have to stop at some point."

The king nodded. "Send Messengers to all the village between here and the next fifty miles. Tell them no one sells a horse to anyone on my orders." The Chief Inquisitor nodded and left the study. The room fell silent again.

The powerlessness killed Quinn, little by little. He felt he must do something, but there was nothing to do. The king had dispatched every resource at his disposal to find Amarice; the Inquisitors and Guards had already made considerable progress.

Quinn thought of Amarice, and his heart ached. He felt an overwhelming sense of fear and tried to remain confident she still lived. He could not imagine a world without her. Elandria could not imagine a world without her; no Sage had ever been attacked before. The country had just passed three centuries of complete peace. What would the kidnapping of the Sage begin? He felt guilty, for not escorting her to her room. And most significantly, he felt helpless that he could do nothing to save the woman he loved.

The clocked ticked; another hour passed. The prince began pacing and swearing under his breath again. The king busied himself with writing correspondence, stopping every few minutes to sigh and press his hands to his eyes. Quinn just turned the diadem over and over in his hands.

The Chief Inquisitor returned shortly before ten o'clock. "A farmer saw the wagon pass his fields at the edge of the Southern Moorlands early this morning. They are headed southeast. On fast horses, we can catch up with them in less than a day and a half."

The king and Raymond began planning a search party. Raymond and the Chief Inquisitor would lead it. They would take a party of twenty on Messenger horses who were fit to travel long distances without stopping. They began naming which guards and Inquisitors they would take with them. When they finished their discussion, Quinn spoke for the first time in hours.

"I'm going, too." The three men looked at him. He had not asked, but told the king that he would be joining the search party. Raymond looked offended.

"No, lad." The king's voice was soft. "I think it best you stay here."

Quinn shook his head. "I need to be there."

Raymond spoke. "Quinn, you have no combat training, no experience with anything like this. You'll be more of a hindrance than a help. We don't need to protect a second person."

Anger flew over Quinn. The woman he loved more than anything was out there, hurting and possibly on her way to some fate that Quinn did not want to imagine. He stared at the prince, silently challenging him. Raymond shifted his posture unconsciously to seem taller, more intimidating. The fire crackled.

Without removing his glare, Quinn lifted a hand toward the fireplace. The flames roared out of the hearth and into the study. He kept the flames balanced in the air, moving them in a controlled circle of fire, then sent them back in the fireplace.

"I think I can handle myself."

The king and the prince gaped. The Chief Inquisitor looked frightened. He spoke first. "Brigitte's tit. My boy, did you just threaten the prince?"

Shit, Quinn thought. Now I'll end up in a cell while they go find Amarice.

But the king spoke. "Don't be ridiculous, Marcus. He was simply demonstrating that he does not need to wield 'a sword to protect himself." Quinn gave him a grateful nod. "I think you can find a horse for Mr. Atwell."

Raymond told Quinn to change, eat something, and meet them at the stables in an hour. Quinn did, and he found a saddlebag waiting on his horse. Raymond approached him. "Water and food rations. Sugar cubes for the horse. And a healer's kit. Who knows what shape we will find her in? I'm technically a Scholar, but I'm a very weak one, and I was always terrible at medicine. So, the healing falls to you." Quinn nodded. "Can you ride?"

"I grew up on a farm," Quinn replied. "I'm familiar with horses." He mounted the brown mare he had been loaned. Raymond grunted in response and mounted his own horse.

"Let's go," Raymond called to the group. "Hyah!"

Twenty horses thundered from the stables and into the city. They passed through the southern gates and onto the road. Quinn breathed in the air, relieved to have some action to take. He kept pace easily; this horse was fast and strong. The Messenger horses were used to traveling some eighty miles in a day without stopping.

They reached the edge of the southern moorlands by nightfall. "We'll camp here," Raymond ordered. "And be gone at first light." Quinn wanted badly to continue, but there was no use in the dark. They would lose their way and not be able to see any sign of Amarice. The feeling of helplessness returned as he ate the dried meat and stale bread from his pouch. He stayed silent, not joining in the banter of the guards around the fire.

Raymond came to sit next to him. Quinn nodded at him in greeting. He felt they were past the formalities, here in the middle of nowhere at night, looking for Amarice; if they were not, he did not care. The prince said nothing for several minutes. Finally, he spoke.

"I love her, you know." His voice was sad. Quinn turned to look at him. "I kept hoping for years that she would change her mind, that she would agree to marry me. She could be Sage and Princess, and she would rule with me one day. But then," he paused, clearing his throat. "Then I met you. And I knew I had no chance." Quinn opened his mouth to speak, but Raymond held up his hand. "I know, you are not together yet. But she looks at you in a way she never looked at me."

Quinn said nothing and stared into the fire. As the flames danced, he thought of Amarice dancing at the Feast of Fire. It seemed so long ago. He thought of her, last night, as he fastened her necklace and kissed her shoulder, as they danced in the ballroom. A single tear ran down his cheek.

"We'll find her," Raymond said. "We'll find her, and we'll make whoever did this pay."

Quinn nodded once, and Raymond said no more. The guards decided on first watch amongst themselves, and Quinn opened his bedroll. He stared at the millions of stars overhead before falling into a dreamless slumber.

CHAPTER 20

The wagon had only stopped briefly before now. Amarice feigned sleep often, and the kidnappers began to worry she was dying. "She best not die on us," the man she had determined to be the leader threatened the others. "Charles'll kill us." When she did open her eyes the first time, they had gagged her and ceased all conversation. She needed to gather as much information as possible, so she kept her eyes closed most of the trip.

But now, the wagon had been stopped for a while to rest the horse. Before nightfall, they had stopped in a small town to buy a new one. No one would sell them so much as a lame mule. They went one by one into the town, keeping the wagon on the outskirts so no one saw the Sage. They could not find anyone willing to sell or trade horses. By the time the fourth one of them had asked, the townsfolk appeared wary, and they decided to keep going.

It was early the next morning, and the horse could barely walk. The kidnappers decided they were far enough away from Teleah to stop for a few hours. Amarice waited to make sure none of them remained in the wagon before opening her eyes.

She had kept her eyes closed for so long that it took her several minutes to focus. Her head still throbbed. She raised a hand to touch the center of pain; it was sticky with blood. She looked herself over. Her arm was bleeding. She knew she would feel light-headed upon sitting; she appeared to have lost a fair share of blood. The front of her dress was covered in vomit. When had that happened? She wondered. What sort of poison did they give me? By this point, she had also wet herself hours ago, and became aware of her malodor.

Amarice shifted her position and stifled a groan. Everything hurt. It took great effort, but she pulled herself to the side of the wagon and peered over the edge.

She was in moorlands; although she was unsure how long she had initially been unconscious and how long she had slept in spurts since then, she figured they were no more than two-and-a-half days into the journey. That meant, she forced her aching mind to recall her knowledge of geography, she was either west or south of the capital. She felt she would have remembered if they had crossed the River Nyva; it would have been too loud to sleep through. South, she determined.

The four men were about fifty yards away, huddled around a small fire. She peered over the other side of the wagon. A wooded area lay about a hundred yards from her. If she could just sneak over there, maybe she could lose them. Unfortunately, she had not yet dared to sit up, let alone walk in stealth. If I can just get to the ground, I can refill my magic enough to walk. She inched her way up, continually checking to make sure none of the kidnappers looked her way.

She hoisted herself over the edge of the wagon and dropped to the ground. She had to fight off the urge to cry out in pain. She felt a large bruise across her abdomen, likely where the one man had kicked her. She folded over in pain behind the wagon wheel. Please, don't see me, she willed. She focused on pulling the magic from the earth. Though the pain still made her want to cry, she could feel strength returning. She began to crawl toward the wood, filling herself with the Gift of the Earth. Power surged through her veins. She stood and began to run. Just a little further, she thought.

"HEY! COME BACK HERE!"

She continued to run, but the men were faster. The gruff man reached her first and threw her to the ground and kicked her again. She cried out in agony. She had to fight back. She tried to crawl away, but he pulled her hair and dragged her backward. "Come back, you whore!"

Amarice tried to focus. The ground began to shake. "Don't let her cast a spell!" Another called. "Don't let her speak!"

"She's not speaking!" the gruff man yelled back. He kicked her again. Clouds rushed into the area, and the sky turned dark. Thunder rumbled. Amarice pulled away as the man looked up at the sky that had previously been blue. Now was her chance. She made the earth shake, hard, and knocked him to his feet. She held a hand out and green streams of magic flowed from her fingertips. The grass began to grow rapidly, lashing him to the ground like ropes. He screamed, and the others stopped running as they watched their friend struggle.

The grass bound his legs and his chest. Then it grew over his neck, suffocating him. He could no longer scream. Amarice watched as the man turned purple, eyes bulging from his ugly face. She did not stop the grass until he was dead.

The youngest of the men, Blake, screamed and ran the opposite direction. The other two men started toward Amarice. She focused on the earth again, and the ground split, forming a deep crevice. One of the men caught his leg in the crack, and she could hear the bone in his leg snap. He cried out in pain. The other man, the leader, turned toward him, stunned.

Amarice stood and raised her hand to the sky. A bolt of lightning flashed, and struck the man where he lay with his leg broken, screaming in pain. He screamed one last time before he fell silent. His clothes smoked, and he fell forward, leg still stuck. His eyes were open, and red welts spread over his face.

The last man turned to face her, a determined anger on his face. Amarice ran toward the woods. She could feel her strength draining and tried to pull more magic from the earth as her feet pounded hard against the ground. The man drew nearer. She reached the trees. But this was not a wood for hiding, and she had no strength to continue running. She froze, unsure what to do next.

"I'll KILL YOU, YOU DEMON BITCH!"

Amarice's eyes searched her surroundings and caught on a tree. The man would run straight past it. She took two steps nearer and focused all her energy on that tree. Please, she begged silently. The man approached. She had to time this perfectly. She steadied her breathing.

The man slowed, unsure why Amarice stood still. He was wary and took his steps carefully to avoid snapping his leg in any more earthquake cracks. Amarice stood between the trees, her arms raised, pointed at the tree nearest the man, and magic streamed from her hands again. He stopped completely and looked up.

As he did, a branch dropped toward him. From the branch, a vine wrapped itself around the man's neck. He screamed. Amarice raised her arms to the sky. The branch snapped back to its heightened position. She heard a crack.

The evil man's neck had snapped. He dangled in the air, the vine a noose.

Amarice collapsed onto the forest floor.

❧❧❧

"WAIT!" Quinn called. Raymond stopped, signaling the others to stop, as well. He pulled his horse back toward Quinn, who pointed off into the distance. They had ridden for hours, ever since the horseman in the last town had reported four different men seeking to trade horses.

Maybe ten miles away, they could see a small grey storm surrounded by clear blue skies. "Looks like magic to me," Raymond said. "Can she create a storm?" Quinn shrugged. He was unsure what exactly the Sage could do in her immense power. "We will investigate." He took off at a gallop and the rest of the party followed.

Quinn felt a light of hope for the first time since they had set off from the palace. If the random storm was a result of Amarice's magic, that meant she was still alive. He urged the horse to go faster. After a few minutes, he heard Raymond yell, "HALT!" He pulled his horse forward, wondering what on earth would cause Raymond to stop this close to finding the Sage.

A young man ran toward them. "Help me! Help!" He appeared unarmed. Raymond dismounted, and Quinn followed suit. The man seemed grateful to see an armed mount of palace guards, but Quinn felt wary. Raymond placed his hand on the hilt of his sword. "Can you help me?" the man panted.

"With what?" Raymond barked at him.

The man doubled over, out of breath. "We—my friends and I—we've been attacked. One of them is dead." The man pointed at the storm area.

"By who?" the prince asked.

"By... by her."

Quinn stepped closer to the man. "By the Sage?" The man looked up at him, shaking.

"She's evil! A sorceress!"

Smack. Quinn's fist met the man's face, and he crumpled to the ground, unconscious. Raymond looked at him, mouth agape. He heard several of the men behind him laugh. "Nice hit," the prince said. "But we could have gotten more information from him."

"Sorry," Quinn muttered.

"Don't be. I wish I had done it myself." He gestured to a guard. "Tie him up. Someone's going to have to carry him on their horse." Raymond galloped on, and most followed, except for two guardsmen who stayed behind to take care of the kidnapper.

❧

IN THE WOODS, Amarice struggled not to give into the pain. She feared the gruff man's kicks had caused internal bleeding. She touched her stomach lightly, and a bolt of pain shot through her. In addition to her head wound and bleeding arm, a gash on her leg dripped blood.

She forced herself to sit up and triage her wounds. She was determined to get out of here alive. If she could slow the bleeding, she could rest and then find her way to the nearest village. She tore off two strips of her urine- and blood-soaked dress. She tied one tightly around her shin and the other around her arm to stop the bleeding. She touched her head. It had begun to scab. Good.

Water, she thought. She sat and listened, trying to hear any sign of running water. She heard drips behind her. A tree dripped rainwater from her storm onto a stone below. It was not much, but it would do.

She searched the floor of the woods, looking for some useful plant. Melaleuca! She gathered several leaves and chewed them in her mouth.

She crawled toward the natural stone bowl of rainwater, and spit the leaves in the water. She took two wads of the chewed leaves and placed them on her wounds to stave off infection. Then she cupped her hands and drank the pitiful excuse of melaleuca tea she had made. She was beyond thirsty and swore she had never tasted anything that delicious.

Doing all she could do to save herself for the moment, she found a soft bed of leaves and curled up to sleep. As she closed her eyes, she pictured Quinn's face. She hoped she could see him one more time.

⁂

THE SEARCH PARTY reached the storm in minutes. A few men drew their swords, ready to meet combat. But the area was silent. There was no one there. Raymond and Quinn slowed their horses into a walk and went further to investigate. "Oh, my..." The prince's voice trailed.

They first saw the man who had fallen into the crack in the earth. They drew nearer on the horse. The man's leg twisted unnaturally, and his femur protruded from his thigh. The rest of his body had fallen forward. They studied the red scars on his face. "He's been struck by lightning," Quinn observed.

"Can she do that?"

Quinn shrugged. "It appears so." He led his horse to what appeared to be another body covered in grass. "Damn. Raymond! Come here." He stared down in disbelief. Somehow, Amarice had grown grass so rapidly she had suffocated him. Raymond said nothing, his eyes wide in shock. Behind them, the other guardsmen had entered the area, and Quinn heard mutters of incredulity. "Where is she?" Quinn asked the prince.

Raymond looked around. "The woods." They trotted their horses to the treeline. In front of them, a man dangled from a tree at least ten feet off the ground, his neck wrapped in a vine. Amarice had managed to hang this man. Raymond turned to look at Quinn. "Did you know she could do this?"

Quinn shook his head. "I never knew what 'most powerful Sage' meant. I guess she did not need us to fight her enemies."

Raymond just stared at the man swaying in the breeze. "She may be hurt, though." He dismounted and tied his horse to a tree. Quinn did the same, and they walked into the woods. It did not take them long to find her, curled up on a pile of leaves.

"Amarice!" Quinn cried and ran toward her. Please be alive. "Amarice!" He knelt next to her and touched her face. She opened her eyes.

"Quinn," she gasped. And she began to cry.

He took her in his arms. "You're all right now. I'm here. You're safe." He rocked her on the ground until her sobs subsided, enveloping her in the peace of his pale blue light. He studied her, trying to determine her wounds. She had a large scab on her head, and he noticed she had made herself two tourniquets from her dress. He smiled to himself. Of course she did, he thought. Only Amarice could use an incredible amount of magic to kill her attackers while wounded, then try to treat her wounds. He touched the chewed leaves on her arm. She was trying to prevent infection. Amazing.

"I'm bleeding internally," she murmured, voice thick with pain.

"Get the Healer's kit and my water," Quinn told Raymond. Raymond left and returned quickly. "Here, my love, drink this." He gave her the water canteen, and she drank as if she had never drunk before. "Not all of it. I need to give you some poppy tea." He opened the Healer's kit and found the bottle labeled poppy. He poured several drops of the extract in the canteen and gave it back to Amarice. He opened a few other vials to pour onto her wounds, some to soothe, others to fight infection.

"I want to go home, Quinn," Amarice said, tears running down her face.

"I know. We will get you home. We will get you well." She nodded, and he picked her up and carried her to his horse. He lifted her onto the saddle and climbed on behind her. She leaned against his chest. Raymond mounted his horse as well. "We need to get her to the Healer in the nearest town. I don't know how severe her hemorrhaging is yet."

Raymond nodded. He gave orders to his men to bury the bodies and not speak of the magic the Sage had done. With a growing suspicion of earth magic in Elandria, stories of the Sage's magic would do nothing to improve the situation. Then he, Quinn, and Marcus galloped to the nearest town to see the Healer.

The poppy tea lulled Amarice into a painless sleep as Quinn held her close while he led the horse. He worried her hemorrhaging had spread, and she would be unable to be saved. He hoped they had arrived in enough time.

"Please don't die," he whispered into her blood-stained hair. "Please don't leave me."

CHAPTER 21

Amarice stayed in a poppy-induced sleep until they arrived in the small town. The Healer, a middle-aged female Scholar with kind dark eyes to match her skin, had plenty of experience with internal hemorrhaging. "Farm town—lots of horse kicks," she told Quinn. She and her assistant took Amarice into a back room. Raymond left briefly to send word to the palace. Quinn paced the front room of the Healer's small home nervously.

After an hour or so, the Healer came to update Quinn. "She will be fine. She needs to stay on poppy tea for at least a week." The Healer had let out some of the bleeding to relieve the pressure, but it appeared to be localized and would cease on its own. They had bathed her, cleaned her wounds, and put her in a fresh gown. "She's sleeping. You can go see her. She will be stable enough to ride in a carriage to the capital tomorrow."

Quinn entered the room. Amarice lay on the single bed, sleeping peacefully under a handmade quilt. He smiled, relieved. The poppy tea would keep her stable so her body could heal on its own. He sat on the bed and stroked her hair. The prospect of losing her had hit Quinn hard, harder even than losing Rafe. He knew without a doubt that he could not live without her. Or, if he did, it would be a shell of an existence. He loved her with every ounce of his being. Even if she did not return his love, he would have to stay near her.

Prince Raymond entered the room quietly. His eyes were red. He, too, had almost lost someone so dear to him. "She'll be all right?" he asked, as if he did not believe the Healer. Quinn nodded and continued to stroke her hair. "Good. I hired a carriage to take us back tomorrow. She can rest at the palace until she's well."

"Did you send word to the Villa? I know they must be worried."

Raymond shook his head. "No, I will do that soon."

The Healer entered the room with two bowls of stew. "Eat, my dears. Nothing better for emotional trauma than a full belly of warm food." She handed them each a bowl and left them alone again. Raymond said no more. He finished his stew and left the room. Quinn sat on the floor next to Amarice and ate a few bites, but he was exhausted. He lay his head on the mattress and fell asleep.

⚜

THE PALACE HEALER kept Amarice asleep on poppy tea for a week until the signs of internal bleeding had stopped and the gashes on her body had turned a healthy shade of pink. Though Quinn was relieved she was well, he missed the sound of her voice, her smile.

He thought back over the last week. They had left the small town in a hired carriage. Amarice had slept the entire journey back to the palace, her head placed on Quinn's lap. She woke briefly upon arrival. The king himself had rushed out to see for himself that she was alive. He looked as if he had not slept in days; indeed, he probably had not.

They had laid the Sage in her normal guest room, and both the palace Healer and the Chief Healer of Teleah had attended to her. Quinn stayed by her side the entire time, leaving only to visit the baths or when the Healers bathed Amarice. Whenever she stirred, they gave her more tea to drink and a bite of food, and then she would fall back into a healing slumber. The king ordered a lounger to be placed next to her bed so Quinn could get some sleep.

Raymond had brought Quinn updates and taken many of his meals in the room with Quinn. The young man they had captured, Blake, had proven a reticent prisoner. He swore only that the Sage and all magic practitioners were evil and must answer for their sins. To whom they must answer, he would not say. The prison guards reported hearing him pray to several gods they had never heard of for protection and forgiveness for his failure. The kidnapper had night terrors from watching Amarice strangle his friend with grass; he woke every night screaming about her evil power.

AMARICE FINALLY WOKE mid-morning on a particularly bright, sunny day. Quinn reclined on the chaise, reading. "Quinn," he heard Amarice murmur in a thick, groggy voice. He leapt up and knelt at her bedside.

"I'm here, I'm right here." He took her hand. Her eyes were still closed, but a smile spread over her face. She slowly opened her eyes to look at Quinn.

"G'morning," she mumbled. Quinn laughed. She squeezed her eyes closed again, then opened them wide, trying to gain her bearings. "Izzit morning?" she asked, voice still thick from the poppy.

"Barely. You are at the palace. You have been asleep for a week, but you appear to be well." He squeezed her hand, unsure how long he would be able to stay affectionate with her now that she was awake.

Her sleepy eyes widened. "A week?" She pulled herself up to sitting and groaned. "No wonder I'm achy." Quinn updated her on what had transpired over the last week. She nodded, taking in all the information. All she could say was, "My magic is drained. I need to take a walk in the gardens."

He nodded. "I will get the Healer. She can help you get dressed and make sure you are well." He paused. "Amarice... your earth magic. We had no idea—"

A single tear ran down her face. "Do you think less of me? I did not use my Gift for good."

"Oh, my lady Sage." He wiped away her tear with his thumb. "I could never think less of you. And you used your Gift to protect yourself. What purpose does the Gift serve if not to keep you safe?" He smiled at her and handed her a cup of water. "I will fetch the Healer. Don't get up."

Quinn smiled at her and left the room. Amarice raised her gown to examine her wounds. The gash on her leg had healed nicely, although she felt certain she would have a lifelong scar. Her abdomen had barely any bruising left, just a small scar where the first Healer had drained some of the blood. She touched it, and felt no pain, and tried to remember that Healer. Everything after Quinn found her felt like a distant memory, clouded by a week's worth of poppy tea. She certainly had no recollection of arriving at the palace.

Quinn. What did it say about her that the first words she uttered in a week were his name? She had not even been sure he was there; she had not been sure where he was. But she said his name, and he answered. She would have to think about this later; for now, she needed to replenish her magic and find out what information the king had about her kidnappers. She stretched and stood, despite Quinn telling her to stay in bed until the Healer arrived. She was surprised to find she felt fine, just a bit weak.

The palace Healer, an older woman named Francis, knocked and entered the room. "My lady Sage, I'm so happy to see you awake." Amarice smiled and allowed Francis to assess her health. "You look well. I imagine you would love a bath."

"More than anything at this moment," Amarice replied. She allowed the Healer to help her to the baths and plunged herself into the warm, perfumed water, relishing its cleansing and pulling some magic from the element. She washed her hair, flinching slightly at the wound on the top of her head. Francis sat, waiting, while Amarice enjoyed scrubbing herself clean. It was not just the wounds and the poppy-induced tea she washed away; it was the feelings of fear and anger, the longing she had to return to Quinn, the memory of her impending death.

Amarice rose from the waters, and Francis handed her a warm towel. "My lady, may I speak to you of something personal?"

Amarice laughed. "Francis, you have known me too long to address me so formally, and too well to ask if you can be personal with me. What is on your mind?"

Francis smiled. "The lad, Quinn. He did not leave your side for a week. I saw the fear in his eyes when you arrived at the palace, heard it in his voice. He did not fear losing the Sage. He feared losing you." She paused, looking for some sign of emotion on Amarice's face; but Amarice was far too good at hiding her thoughts. "Amarice, that boy loves you with a rare sort of love. I just thought you should know."

Amarice smiled, though her eyes revealed nothing. "Thank you, Francis. I think I would like to get dressed now."

QUINN STOOD outside her room when Amarice returned from the baths. "Feel better?" he asked her with a grin, pure happiness shining in his eyes. A flood of emotions rushed over Amarice, but she forced herself to reveal nothing. She smiled back, cautious not to reveal too much to the man who sat at her bedside constantly for the last week. Now was not the time.

"Infinitely. I'd like to take a walk in the gardens, though. My magic is drained." Quinn offered to escort her. "No, I need to be alone with my thoughts. I'll be fine," she added, addressing the concern that spread over his face.

When she returned from her walk, magic once again flowing through her veins, Quinn was still standing outside her door. "The king wants to see you, if you are up for it." Amarice agreed, and together they walked to the king's study. Quinn walked two steps behind her, and the air hung heavy between them with unsaid words.

King Roland greeted her with a warm, fatherly embrace. "Oh, Amarice. I have barely slept with worry. You look well." He hugged her again, as if convincing himself she really stood before him, alive and healthy. "How do you feel?"

"Tired, but I have no pain. The Healers did their work well."

The king nodded. "And Quinn. From what Raymond said, he performed excellent triage when he found you." Amarice turned to smile at her apprentice and noticed for the first time how heavy with worry and exhaustion his eyes were. He returned her smile.

Quinn brushed aside the comment with humility. "I don't think we're giving the Sage enough credit, your highness. When I arrived, she had already begun to treat her wounds with melaleuca. I'm sure few people in that condition would have been able to do what she did to stay alive."

Amarice bit her lip, unsure what to say. The memory of crawling on the forest floor in pain and chewing the melaleuca leaves came flooding back. She would have let herself collapse in agony if not for the thought of returning to Quinn. She had not fought for her life to fulfill her duties as Sage, but instead to see Quinn again. Now that she no longer faced death, her fear of love and heartbreak had returned in earnest.

For the moment, at least, she needed to be the Sage. "Have you learned anything about the attackers? I know they were taking me to a man named Charles to 'answer for my sins' as they put it."

The king shook his head. "The prisoner will not speak much. He prays to two gods and a goddess. We did not know about this Charles; I will inform the Chief Inquisitor that we have a name." The king took a seat behind his desk. A look of fear passed over his face. "Amarice. These men that took you. What did they... How did they...?" He could not finish his sentence.

Amarice looked confused. Quinn clarified. "My lady," he said with an odd formality to hide his emotion. "We have wondered whether they—took advantage of you. In the worst way."

For the first time, Amarice sat on the sofa. Quinn remained standing. Rape was punishable by death in Elandria. But that was not why these two men looked concerned; they had feared greatly for her safety. Amarice sighed. "No." She replayed the conversations of her kidnappers in her mind. "The one you have in the cells... he wanted to. He was rather obscene. But the others warned him my evil would rub off on him." She laughed a dark laugh. "Good thing I am evil, I suppose."

Anger flashed over Quinn's face. She looked away, unable to bear the emotions he kept revealing despite his best efforts. She spoke again, matter-of-factly informing the king what else she had learned. Charles, whoever he was, was behind the other attacks. The men had said they would arrive in three days' time if they had been able to get a new horse. Surely the Inquisitor could learn something from that.

"I want to see the prisoner." For the first time since waking, Amarice slipped into her authority as the Sage. The king opened his mouth to protest, but she fixed him with a stony stare. He nodded.

"Raymond will return from Parliament soon. I will have him escort you down to the cells."

Amarice thanked him and took her leave to rest until Raymond returned. Quinn followed her in silence. When they reached their rooms, she told Quinn to rest on his own bed and promised to wake him before visiting the prisoner. Then she disappeared into her room.

⚜

QUINN LAY ON HIS BED, unable to sleep. Tears of relief ran down his face. Though the Healers had assured him she would recover, a part of him feared he would never see her again. And the first word she had uttered in a week was his name. His heart ached. He wanted to take her in his arms, to kiss her soft lips. But she had just been through a terrible trauma. He would wait.

An hour passed before he heard a knock. He wiped his wet face and smoothed his hair before opening the door. Raymond and Amarice stood before him. "Let's go see the bastard," Raymond said. Amarice said nothing, her face expressionless.

"Just a moment," Quinn said. He stepped further inside to the dresser and took something from the top. "My lady, I think you lost something." He handed her the Sage's diadem, freshly cleaned and polished by the king's jeweler. No trace of blood remained on the silver; the gems sparkled.

Amarice gave him a smile and took the diadem from Quinn. She studied it, turning it over in her hands. She had not given a thought to it at all. There were times she hated being the Sage. It was lonely and came with a responsibility to millions of people that she did not always want. But in this moment, her power flooded through her veins with fury. One of the men targeting both sets of her people sat in a prison cell floors below them, a man with answers. A man who feared her for her power. Good, she thought. Let him be scared. She placed the diadem atop her head, and felt herself stand taller, stronger.

Quinn and Raymond stared at her. Her beauty was immense, her power more so. She straightened her diadem and rolled back her shoulders. She gave no sign that she had just woken from a poppy-sleep, no sign that a week ago, she had been found bleeding in the woods. And though in their presence, she usually put on no ceremony, in this moment, both men knew beyond a shadow of a doubt that this was the most powerful person to ever live.

She gave them a terrifying grin and a wink. "Now we can go see the miscreant." Raymond led the Sage and her apprentice down to the prison cells. Below the palace, the ancient catacombs were dark and lined with flaming torches. The stone walls dripped with moisture. Quinn had to duck through many of the walkways, though the prince and the Sage had no issues.

A feeling of apprehension settled over Quinn. With the open flames on the wall, he worried his magic would fly out of control. The last time he had seen this man, he had knocked him into unconsciousness. But then he saw what they had done to Amarice. He felt a primitive urge to rip the man to shreds; indeed, he had imagined killing the bastard many times over the last week.

They turned a corner, and the prison guards greeted the Sage with awe. She gave only a curt nod in response. The image of Amarice's destruction flooded Quinn's mind. She doesn't need anyone to kill him for her, he thought. But the protective urge did not go away.

Raymond grabbed a torch from the wall and stopped at the end of a dark tunnel. "Wake up, you piece of shit," he said to the prisoner inside the cell. There was no princely decorum in his voice. "You've got a visitor."

"I already said I won't talk!" the man cried.

Amarice stepped to the front of the cell; Quinn followed. The prisoner screamed at the sight of her. "SORCERESS! DEMON!"

"Oh, stop that awful noise," the Sage commanded with a sharp authority. To Quinn's surprise, the man stopped screaming. "Tell me about Charles." The man whimpered, but he shook his head no. Amarice fixed him in her gaze. "Fine. I'll tell you what I think. You can tell me if I'm right." She paused, waiting for a response. "Blake, I think you were a nice man, once. Nice, but weak. You had no power, no one took you seriously. And then you met a man named Charles. And Charles was kind and vibrant, and he understood you. You and all the other weak, powerless men. Charles convinced you that you were strong, and that the Scholars and the Deyoni had taken your rightful power as men." She studied the man in front of her who quivered in fear. "How am I doing?"

"You're evil, sinner," he managed to say, though his voice shook.

"Oh, yes. You poisoned me, kidnapped me, and beat me. You planned to deliver me to be tortured and killed. But I'm the one with the questionable morals. Of course." Behind her, Quinn stifled a laugh. The prisoner ducked his head. "Where was I?" she asked. "Oh, yes. Charles convinced you that men had the rightful power over the earth, over women, over the Parliament in Teleah, over everything. And you believed him. Because he validated your insecurity. And for him, you would do anything."

At this point, she knelt to the ground in front of the man to look him straight in the eyes. The man shook violently in fear. "Let me be clear, Blake. You are weak. You are powerless. And you always will be. You let some man make decisions for you, letting you believe you had some sort of power over the world. But really he had power over you." She touched her hand to the ground, and the earth began to shake, rattling the metal bars of the cells. The man cried out in terror. "You have no power. No one has power over the earth. The earth has power over us. Yes, even me. Where do you think our magic comes from? You are nothing more than a speck of life that the earth allows to live." She removed her hand from the ground, and the catacombs stopped shaking. "Remember that. And if you decide to tell the guards where to find Charles, you will regain some semblance of the decency you once had."

Amarice stood, took the torch from Raymond, and walked away. Quinn took one last glance at the man, then turned to follow her. The guards looked at the Sage in wonder as she handed them the torch at the end of the tunnel. She said nothing the entire walk back to the rooms. As she reached the door, she said, "We return home tomorrow," then disappeared into her room.

Raymond and Quinn stood in the hallway, looking at each other, unsure what to make of the situation. Quinn cleared his throat. "There's a reason she's the Sage, isn't there?"

Raymond laughed. "I don't know about you, my friend. But I have never been more terrified or aroused as I was in the catacombs just now." He laughed again, shaking his head and walked away without a goodbye.

Quinn knew exactly what he meant.

CHAPTER 22

The carriage left the city through the northern gates, and Amarice breathed a sigh of relief. Home was just a few hours away. She looked out the window, staring at the town and the countryside beyond. The day had dawned bright and cloudless. The summer sun shone high in the sky, and the trees and grasses were the greenest Quinn had ever seen. Soon, the air would grow crisper and the leaves would begin to change. But today, the sun matched his mood: he, too, was glad to be returning to the Villa. He was glad Amarice sat before him on the carriage seat, healthy and glowing.

He watched her as she stared out the window. She had swept her unpinned hair over her left shoulder, leaving her right shoulder bare. She wore a dress the color of the summer leaves, thin and gauzy, gathered behind her neck. She had placed the Sage's diadem in her satchel the moment the carriage had left the palace. For the first time in what seemed like an eternity, she was just Amarice again.

The town gave way to the colorful Deyoni camps. Today, no crowds of Deyoni ran alongside the carriage. Amarice had requested an unmarked carriage to avoid the attention. "I just want to get home in peace," she had told the king.

An hour passed before Amarice spoke. "The Healer said you

never left my side." Quinn shifted uncomfortably. He wanted Amarice, but he did not want to rush her after what she had been through. And she had previously rejected him. Twice. He opted to say nothing and waited for her to continue. "Why?" she asked after several moments.

He sighed. "Do you not know, Amarice?"

She turned her head from the window and met his eyes. "After everything these last few months, you still love me?"

"Oh, Amarice. I love you more with every passing day." She dropped her eyes to her lap and fiddled her thumbs. "And I think you love me, as well."

She kept her eyes turned downward. "Of course, I do. But..." Her voice trailed. He deserved an explanation of her inhibitions. After all he had done for her, after keeping vigil at her side. "Quinn, I love you too much to take you into my bed only to have you leave in a few months' time." She forced herself to look at his face, but it hurt too much. She dropped her gaze again.

Quinn looked confused for a moment, then a smile spread across his face. He laughed. Amarice's jaw dropped at his response. "What?" she asked, taken aback.

"You are the most powerful Sage to ever walk the earth. You can have any lover you choose. And you are afraid I'm going to break your heart? Me?" He laughed again. The Sage was afraid this shy, inexperienced young man was going to hurt her.

"Well... yes."

He stopped laughing and his face softened. He reached across the carriage and took her small hand in his strong one. "Amarice. I will not break your heart." A tear ran down her cheek. "Look at me, my love." She turned her wet eyes to meet his warm, brown gaze. "I will not break your heart." And she believed him.

He leaned forward and wiped her tears with his thumb. She brought her face closer to him and tentatively set her lips on his. He parted his lips in response, and she kissed him with more confidence. He met her kiss with vigor and ran his hand through her hair.

Quinn pulled her across the carriage, and she straddled his lap in the carriage seat. He breathed in her scent as they kissed, getting drunk off her intoxicating presence. She nibbled his lip, and he grew hard underneath her. She giggled seductively.

He moved his mouth to her neck, and she moaned in response. He ran his hands over her bare spine to the top of her neck, where he unfastened her dress. It fell over her, revealing her supple breasts. Quinn kissed her neck and worked his way lower. She cried out in pleasure.

Amarice rocked her hips back and forth over his erection. She had never wanted anyone more than she wanted him in this instant. She moved her hands under his shirt, rubbing his chest, before she decided he did not need to be wearing it a moment longer. She tugged the shirt over his head. Now beautifully bare-chested, he returned his attention again to kissing her.

When she could take it no longer, she shifted enough to unlace his pants and reveal his manhood. He groaned in her ear. She gathered the skirt of her dress in one hand, and he lifted her onto him, moaning loudly at her wet warmth that covered his hardness.

She rode him, seated, as the carriage continued to draw closer to the mountains. But neither gave any thought to where they were. The only thing that existed was the two of them, finally together as one. She placed one hand on his chest, over his heart, as he kissed her. She moved her hips up and down, relishing the feeling finally being one.

Quinn wound his fingers in her hair as she sped up her rhythm. Nothing had ever felt so right, so perfect as Amarice on top of him. His breathing quickened. She went faster, moaning, until her body quaked and she cried out in ecstasy. Quinn ran his hands down her spine and lifted her buttocks still faster until he thought he would burst in pure euphoria. He, too, cried out in pleasure as he spilled himself inside of her, months of desire releasing into the woman he adored.

Amarice kissed him softly. She stayed in his lap, and he wrapped his arms around her, pulling her close. She laid her head against his chest, her breaths slowing. Quinn breathed in the flowery scent of her hair as he ran one hand over her back. He closed his eyes. This was how it was supposed to be.

After several minutes, Amarice pulled her head away and smiled at him, eyes glazed from pleasure. "I love you, Quinn Atwell."

"I love you, Amarice Teyvana, Sage of Elandria." He smiled as he caressed her cheek. "I love you, and I realized this week I cannot be without you."

She pulled herself off him, then laid across the carriage seat, head in his lap. "In the woods, my biggest fear, my only fear, was that I would never see you again." He stroked her hair, and she felt safe. She yawned.

He placed one hand on her stomach and touched the small scar where the first Healer had let out her hemorrhaging. He remembered how scared he had felt as he paced the Healer's front room, and he hoped he would never feel that fear of losing her ever again. "Sleep, my love. You're safe."

She closed her eyes. Quinn watched her as she drifted into sleep, studying her perfect features. The horses trotted steadily toward the Villa, and the movement lulled Quinn into sleep. He leaned his head against the wall of the carriage and drifted into a peaceful slumber, the woman he loved under his arms.

⚘

THE CARRIAGE STOPPED ABRUPTLY, jolting both Quinn and Amarice awake. Quinn glanced out the window as Amarice squinted, trying to regain her senses. "Amarice, we're home," Quinn said. Amarice shook herself to wake up and retied her dress behind her neck. "Where's my shirt?" he asked her.

She looked at him blankly for a moment then began to laugh hysterically. He grinned at the ridiculousness of the situation, as well, and fumbled for his shirt. The carriage driver opened the door as Quinn pulled the shirt over his head. Amarice lost it again at the expression on the driver's face. "Sorry," muttered Quinn, turning a light shade of pink.

The driver said nothing as he helped the Sage down the carriage steps. Quinn followed, carrying both of their bags. He turned around to look at the mountains that he called home, breathing in the fragrant summer air. Amarice had stopped laughing as she, too, turned to take in the beauty of the Sage's Mountains and the glistening stone expanse of the Villa. Tears ran down her face. "I missed it so much," she whispered. Quinn placed a hand on her shoulder in comfort. She sighed, composing herself. "Come," she said. "Let's go see the family."

As they entered the garden, Madge ran out of the Villa, shrieking and crying. She threw her arms around Amarice. The rest of the permanent residents and the visiting Scholars made their way into the garden to greet their mistress. Daisy's red hair trailed behind her as she ran through the courtyard and out the main doors. She pushed Madge aside and pulled her dear friend into a strong embrace.

Madge then threw her arms around Quinn in the way only a motherlike figure could. "I'm glad you're home safe, my boy," she sobbed. Quinn returned the embrace with love. For the first time in his life, he felt he really belonged: here, with Amarice and the others who considered him family. He swallowed, determined not to cry.

Everyone greeted them with hugs and well-wishes. Finally, Madge yelled at everyone to make room so Amarice could come inside. "You must be exhausted, my dears. Are you hungry?" The head-of-house barked at two servants to take Quinn and Amarice's satchels and fetch something to eat. Madge wrapped her arm through the Sage's and took her to the salon. The regular residents followed, glad to once more be in her presence.

One of the maids brought in crusty bread and cheese. It occurred to Quinn that they had missed lunch, although the palace cook had sent them with a basket of food. He smiled to himself as he remembered the course their journey had taken, shoving a huge bite of bread into his mouth to distract his thoughts.

Amarice finished eating and stood. "Madge, I think I would like to go to bed. I hope you do not take offense at my abrupt departure."

Madge hugged Amarice close one more time. "Of course not, my dear. I'm just glad you are home safely where you belong." The older woman dabbed at her eyes with the corner of her apron.

"Me, too." Amarice began to cross the room. Quinn sat, unsure what to do. He wanted to follow her, but she was heading to her private quarters. He watched her hips sway as she walked. Suddenly, she stopped and turned to meet Quinn's eyes. "Are you coming, Quinn?"

Quinn stood to the sound of Daisy's audible gasp. Heat crept into his face. He felt like he was trudging through mud; the walk across the salon seemed infinitely longer with everyone's stares. Amarice never took anyone into her chambers. "Finally," he heard someone mutter. He reached Amarice and placed one hand on the small of her back, and together they left the room.

She said nothing as they walked through her study. At the door to her chambers, she paused, smiling at Quinn. He could only stare at her beauty, barely believing that she was his. She opened the door, and he stepped inside, glimpsing a piece of Amarice that no one ever saw.

The first floor held a small living area with an overstuffed chair and a chaise lounge covered with a raggedy blanket that had once been vibrantly colored. Skylights allowed in the sun and gave life to the plants she kept inside. Bookshelves lined the walls, and the books were placed with no order. Pieces of parchment and opened books lined every open surface. A dress hung over the back of a chair at a small table. Quinn had never once considered whether Amarice was neat or untidy. A quick urge to straighten the room flashed over him. He pushed it aside and smiled at the woman in front him; the woman who was no longer the stuff of myths, but instead the woman who loved him.

Amarice took his hand and led him up the staircase to her bedroom. Inside, Quinn saw the biggest bed he had ever seen. It was covered in bright pillows and lush blankets. He noticed it was unmade. He grinned. Another lounge sat opposite the bed, and it was covered in her dresses, despite the three large wardrobes that lined the wall. A stack of books sat on a nightstand. Thick purple curtains covered the door to her balcony.

He took in everything, the significance of being allowed in here not at all lost on him. Then he pulled Amarice close and kissed her fiercely. She threw her arms around his neck, parting her lips in earnest. He untied her dress again, and it fell to the floor. He broke away, studying her naked body in all its beauty. She bit her lip, then knelt to the floor to unlace his pants. After a few moments, he was undressed, over six feet of perfect man. She led him to her bed.

They spent the next several hours learning each other's bodies. When they finally stopped to rest, Amarice lay in his arms. "Quinn?"

"Hmm?" He was love-drunk and barely coherent.

"I have too many wardrobes." He looked at her, puzzled at her idea of pillow talk. "I just mean, if you wanted to move your belongings in here, I have plenty of room."

Quinn propped himself on his elbow to look in her eyes. "Is the Sage asking me to move in with her?"

She looked embarrassed, which only endeared her to him more. "Only if you want to. I mean, I don't really want to spend a night without you by my side, so it just seems as if it would make more sense to keep your things in here."

He chuckled and kissed her. "It makes perfect sense." And he pulled her on top of him once again. Tomorrow, they could combat the evil that had infiltrated their peaceful country. But for today, they would simply be together, wrapped in each other's arms, and overcome by love.

CHAPTER 23

Quinn's pure happiness lasted for a week. Every morning, he woke to Amarice in his arms and made love to her before breakfast. Every day, they spent in each other's company, sharing the parts of themselves they had never told another soul. And every night, he worshipped her in their bed before kissing her goodnight.

But after a week, a Messenger arrived from the palace while the Villa residents ate lunch. Amarice offered the young lady Messenger a place at the table before opening the letter. Quinn smiled, wondering how Amarice could continue to be even more amazing than the day before. Then he noticed her face change into a look of panic. "Amarice? What is it?"

She handed him the letter, eyes wide, and called for Madge. Quinn quickly scanned the letter; the king was arriving at the Villa the day after tomorrow. He had news about the man named Charles. At first Quinn thought Amarice looked panicked over news of her attackers; then he scanned the table and remembered the twenty additional Scholars who currently stayed at the Villa.

"Quinn, I cannot... it's too much..."

Madge bustled into the veranda at that moment, startled by

Amarice's panicked cry. Quinn handed her the letter. The head-of-house met the Sage's eyes. "How on earth are we going to fit that many people here?" Amarice shrugged and tears rolled down her face. The trauma was too fresh to deal with the task of preparing for a royal visit. Madge looked as if she might cry. The rest of the table looked on at the two women.

Quinn spoke. "Get everyone in here. We will make it work." Madge nodded and went to collect the Scholars and house staff who were not at lunch. Amarice sat back down and buried her head in her hands. Quinn patted her back in reassurance. He could not help but smile to himself. The woman had used extraordinarily powerful magic to kill three attackers, but she found herself flustered at preparing her home for the king.

Once the entire residency of the Villa had made their way to the veranda, Quinn took charge in explaining the situation. Many offered to double up their rooms for a few nights, and several offered to go visit the capital. He made sure everyone took on some responsibility of preparing the Villa, then sent everyone on their way to pack up and clean their rooms.

"Thank you," Amarice whispered with grateful eyes. "I'm not quite up to mundane details, and the Villa has never been so full." She squeezed his hand.

He leaned in to kiss her forehead. "Anything for you." He finished his lunch without saying much, musing on how his role had shifted. Taking charge had never been a skill of his, but he had stepped up without a thought. He spent the rest of the afternoon and the next day answering questions from Scholars and house staff. Somehow, he had become an authority in the house. Every time it felt too surreal, he kissed Amarice.

By the time the king arrived, the Villa sparkled, and rooms were prepared for the royal company. Amarice had rewarded Quinn generously for his leadership; he had struggled to remove himself from the bed and could not keep his thoughts appropriate all morning. Amarice, on the other hand, had become withdrawn since breakfast. He knew she worried about the king's news, whether she would admit it or not. He stayed close to her, placing a hand on her back or a kiss on her cheek to assure her she would not face the news alone.

The king arrived with no pomp and circumstance. One palace carriage pulled in front of the Villa, and a handful of armed guards rode in on horses. Everyone from the Villa spanned the garden to greet King Roland on his arrival. Scholars chattered in excitement at the prospect of meeting the king. Quinn marveled at how unexciting it was now to see Roland, and once again fought off a feeling of surrealism.

Amarice stood at the edge of the garden with Quinn. The driver opened the carriage door. The Chief Inquisitor stepped out first, followed by the prince. Quinn placed a hand on Amarice's hip without thinking; though he liked the prince, and they had shared much during Amarice's kidnapping and recovery, he could not help the twinge of jealousy. Amarice did not move, allowing his hand to rest where it lay.

The king stepped out of the carriage, royal blue traveling clothes stretched tight over his belly. Quinn had not noticed how much weight the man had acquired recently and realized the attacks had taken their toll on more than just Amarice and himself. Roland smiled upon seeing Amarice, but he could not hide the stress and exhaustion in his eyes.

The king grabbed Amarice in a strong hug. "You look well, my dear," he told her. Then he turned to Quinn and embraced him. "I assume you have taken good care of her, yes?"

Quinn choked on his response; Amarice kicked his shin. He looked at her holding back her laughter. "He has, my King," she managed to say. She greeted Raymond and Marcus. "Shall we adjourn to my study? My head-of-house can show your guards to their rooms." The king nodded, and Amarice turned to lead them through the Villa to her study. Out of newly found habit, Quinn placed his hand on her back, then removed it quickly. He looked around and met Raymond's eyes. The prince raised an eyebrow.

In the study, Amarice offered the king the plush chair behind her desk. He refused and sat next to his son and the Inquisitor on a sofa. Quinn sat opposite to them, and to his surprise, Amarice sat directly next to him and placed a hand in his lap. Hesitantly, he moved his arm over her shoulders, and she leaned into him. The Sage of Elandria gave no thought as to what other people thought of her and had no reason to hide her relationship, even in the presence of royalty.

"Well, what news brings you to the Villa, my King?" Amarice asked. She did not have the air of Sage about her; she was at home, and here she was simply Amarice, even with the king sitting in front of her. The king inclined his head toward the Chief Inquisitor.

Marcus spoke. "Whatever you said to the prisoner worked, my lady. He sobbed constantly for a few days, but then he asked to speak to the prince. He told us where to find the man Charles." He gestured to Raymond.

"Charles Chambers holds church every day of the week in a village about a week's journey from here. From what we can gather, he appears to have come out of nowhere. He preaches about the dominance of men over women and the evils of magic, as you suspected." Raymond cleared his throat. "The religion appears to be similar to other rural religions: there is a patron god, a mother goddess, and a punisher god."

Quinn nodded. His own upbringing had taught him of a manifestation of those deities, along with a couple minor ones. And though his village had a suspicion of magic and hatred of the Deyoni, they had never preached outright attacks.

Amarice said what he thought. "Yes, but no other village church has engaged in widespread attacks across Elandria."

The Inquisitor nodded. "The man must be deranged, but incredibly charismatic. The prisoner and his comrades that kidnapped you—" Amarice tensed, and Quinn squeezed her close—"were not directly involved in the other attacks. But men were promised absolution and reward for engaging in various works under Chambers' orders."

The king spoke for the first time. "He sent men into villages across Elandria to place seeds of doubt and spread propaganda. We must go after Charles."

"Yes, Father, you're right," said Raymond. "But getting rid of Charles does not get rid of the problem. Who knows how much deeper this goes than a few attacks?"

It was Quinn's turn to tense, and the memory of Rafe's death came flooding back. Amarice took his hand in hers. The king responded to Raymond, "But without his leadership..."

"Without his leadership, he has still planted thoughts of evil throughout the country! Ideas last longer than people, Father!" Raymond had leaped from his seat in anger. He took a deep breath and sat back down on the sofa. "Forgive me, Father."

The king gave Raymond a sad smile. "As you can see, Raymond and I have some different ideas about how best to solve the problem. What do you think, my lady Sage?"

Amarice sighed and chewed her lip, thinking. "Raymond is correct, but Chambers must be removed from power if we have any hope of combatting the ideology he has imparted on our people."

"And how do you propose we do remove him from power?" the king asked. Though he could make the call himself, and he could operate outside of Parliament's jurisdiction, he seemed to be asking for the Sage's permission.

Amarice's voice took on the terrifying power that it had in the catacombs. "As far as I am concerned, Charles and his fanatics are directly responsible for the deaths of many of my brethren. I would have him killed." She stood, squeezing Quinn's hand as she did. "But, he has to answer for his crimes in front of Parliament. And I will arrest him myself."

❧

MADGE HAD PREPARED a feast in honor of the king's visit. Quinn had been relegated to the other side of Amarice. Madge had explained that because the Sage and whoever was the ruler were considered political equals, the Sage retained her seat at the head of the table when the king visited. But the king took the position of honor to her left. Quinn was shocked that he was permitted to sit where he was, assuming the prince would sit on the Sage's other side. But Amarice had instructed Madge that Quinn was to sit to her right tonight.

Prince Raymond sat on Quinn's other side. He tried to lighten the mood, but their earlier meeting had turned tense. The king had not wanted Amarice to go after Charles for her safety. Raymond, who had seen the damage Amarice could do with her Gift, had argued vehemently in Amarice's favor. Roland had threatened to use his kingly power to forbid her from going. Amarice assured him she would just go without his permission. Quinn and Marcus had sat quietly until the king addressed them directly.

"She will not be alone," Quinn had told him. "Not that she needs any help, but I have a fair amount of power myself."

"My King, I saw what her power can do," the Inquisitor had agreed. "As long as no one slips her poison in her drink again, she is far more dangerous than a cavalry."

"I'm right here!" Amarice had cried. "If you could talk about me as if I am in the room and as if I am the Sage of Elandria, it would be much appreciated." She had muttered something under her breath about men, but finally the king agreed. He insisted that Amarice and Quinn would be escorted by at least ten royal guards and the Inquisitor. Raymond had then started an argument about going, too. He eventually won.

Therefore, dinner at the far end of the table was tense. Quinn spent an inordinate amount of time slicing his steak and chewing his vegetables, trying to ignore the tension. Further down, though, the dining room was far more cheerful. The younger Scholars enjoyed the company of the handsome palace guards immensely. Quinn felt certain every guard would end up in a Scholar's bed tonight and made a mental note to consider that the next time he had to make sleeping arrangements.

The Villa residents and their guests retired to the parlor after the feast. The king accepted introductions willingly, but he excused himself to bed after a short time. Quinn noticed an enamored palace guard attempting to flirt with Amarice. She indulged him kindly, but kept shooting subtle eye rolls at Quinn across the room.

Raymond, who had been whispering seductively with Daisy in a corner, approached Quinn. "So, you and Amarice finally...?"

Quinn chuckled. "Yes." He did not know what to say next.

Raymond downed the rest of the wine he held in his hand in one gulp. "Promise me you will take good care of her."

"I wouldn't dream of doing anything else." At that moment, Amarice sidled up to them and wrapped her arms around Quinn's waist. He bent down to kiss her. "Finally got away from the poor guard, I see."

She rolled her eyes. "I'm not sure he's ever met a woman before. It was painful."

Raymond snorted, and Quinn squeezed her close. "He's never met a woman like you before. Give the lad a break. You're quite intimidating, you know."

Amarice flashed him a tipsy smile. "I'm ready to retire for the night." She turned to address the prince. "Raymond, you would not be offended if we went to bed, would you?"

"Not at all," he told her, though Quinn heard some strain in his voice. "I was rather enjoying the company of that redhead over there." He jerked his head toward Daisy.

"Oh, you'll have good fun with her," Amarice replied. She winked. "Good night, Raymond." She pulled on Quinn's hand and led him from the parlor and into their quarters. She began to undress as soon as the door was shut and threw her gown on the sofa. Quinn picked it up and folded it to bring upstairs. "Can you believe Roland this afternoon?"

She thundered up the stairs and flung herself into the oversized bed. Quinn followed and placed her dress in the wardrobe. He began to undress, neatly folding his trousers and shirt and placing them on the chaise to be washed later. "He cares about your safety, Amarice. That's all. We all do."

"I can take care of myself," she muttered, her speech slightly slurred from the wine. Quinn climbed into bed next to her and kissed her forehead.

"I know, my love. But you said yourself he is like a father to you. Let him worry. It's a compliment, not an insult."

Amarice sighed and reclined against the pillows. She muttered a few stubborn obscenities before admitting Quinn was right. He laughed at her, and she hit him with a pillow. "Besides, you cannot do everything yourself." She gave him a defiant look until he met her lips with his and shifted to be on top of her.

CHAPTER 24

It felt strange to see Amarice on a horse in traveling clothes, Quinn mused as he rode behind her. It was not that she looked out of place; indeed, she seemed rather at ease on a horse, hair windblown and face dusty from the road. But he had never seen her fall into such an ordinary role. The king had offered her a palace carriage, but Amarice had refused, much to Quinn's chagrin. She was already upset about the number of kings' guard that were accompanying them and felt a carriage might tip off Charles before they arrived.

She was right, of course, but on this third day, Quinn was tired of riding. Every muscle ached, and he wanted to lay on his overstuffed bed for a week. They were at least two days out from Headham, the village in the southern moorlands where Charles Chambers kept church. Though he had grown up riding horses, he had never ventured more than a day's ride from Corthy.

If Amarice felt the same, she did not reveal it. In her posture, her demeanor, Quinn could see her Deyoni blood. She traveled well and looked as beautiful as ever in her flared pantaloons and woven tunic typical of the horse-backed Deyoni women. She laughed heartily at Raymond's inappropriate stories and joked with the kings' guard, who grew more enamored by her each day. More than once, Quinn had approached a group of them and heard their boyish wonderings. They silenced themselves whenever Quinn drew near. On one such occasion, he had simply told them the answer to their question about Amarice was "yes" before riding off with a grin.

The sun beat harshly upon the riders today. Beads of sweat rolled down Quinn's brow, and he hated himself for purchasing dark riding clothes. Amarice tied her hair into a knot on top of her head and took a large drink of water from her canteen. Quinn led his horse into a trot to catch up to her. She handed him her canteen. "Still cold," she told him. He savored the cool, wet liquid as it passed over his throat.

"I miss my dresses," she said. "This is just far too much fabric."

He grinned. "I agree. You should just remove every bit of it." She tried to slap him playfully, but he pulled his horse away and changed the subject. "You look so at ease riding. I suppose I am not so in touch with my Deyoni side as you."

Amarice's laughter rang out on the open road. "I'm just better at faking it than you. Everything aches, and I could fall asleep right this moment." Quinn removed a hand from the reins and reached out to touch her face. She sighed. "We should stop for lunch soon and take a rest." She called out to Raymond, who was several horses ahead of them. The prince turned his horse round and approached them. "Can we stop and rest soon?"

The prince looked around and studied the landscape. He pointed at a distant farmhouse. "There is a shady wood and a small lake on their land. The old woman lets us stop often. I'll send a guard ahead." He rode off to give orders to one of the young men accompanying them.

Quinn was amazed that Raymond could remember any sort of landmarks in the area. To him, everything looked like indistinguishable green moorland and every farm they passed looked the same. But this was the furthest south Quinn had ever visited, and he tried to appreciate that. Even though they were headed to arrest a cult leader, Quinn decided he could enjoy the journey there. A spasm shot through his calf from hours on his horse. I'd enjoy it more in a carriage, he thought to himself.

The company rode their horses to the farm lake and relaxed in the much-needed shade of the conifer woods. Amarice lay flat on her back, soaking in the earth's magic. Quinn sat next to her, replenishing his own well of power. After several minutes, Amarice sat up and leaned her head against Quinn's shoulder. "Are we doing the right thing?" she asked him.

He pulled her onto his lap and wrapped his arms around her waist. "I don't know," he told her honestly. "He cannot be allowed to continue what he is doing."

"He must answer for his crimes. But should he just be killed instead?" She sighed, and Quinn felt the strain of her inner conflict flow through her. He, too, had wondered this. But as leader of the Scholars and the voice of the Deyoni, it was right that she should execute the man's fate according to the laws of the land. Killing him without a trial may give more credence to his cause, and how deeply seated his ideologies ran, they did not know.

"The bastard is responsible for the deaths of dozens of innocent people. He deserves to stand trial and answer for his crimes publicly." He tightened his embrace around her, providing reassurance to the woman who rarely needed anyone else's strength. "We will deal with whatever consequences it brings."

She relaxed a bit in his arms. "We. I like the sound of that."

They did not speak any more of it for the rest of the day, nor the next. The closer they drew to Headham, the quieter they became. Even the guards' jokes and songs subsided into introspection and apprehension. Some had seen the devastation Amarice had left on her kidnappers; the rest had heard the stories. There was no need to exaggerate what the Sage was capable of doing. And they headed into an unknown situation to confront the man who had brought so much darkness into Elandria over the past year.

The company set up camp ten miles from Headham. Tomorrow brought uncertainty, and the mood at camp was heavy. Raymond reviewed the plan with everyone, then retired early to his tent. Quinn played with the flames of the cooking fire mindlessly, drawing them out and making them dance in circles before sending them back to the fire. Amarice watched the dancing flames as if she expected them to give her some sort of guidance or answer. Finally, she spoke. "Let's go to bed."

Quinn put out the fire with his magic. The night was muggy, and they did not need the heat. He followed her into their tent and began to undress. She pulled her lightweight shift over her head and sat on her bedroll, then fell into sobs.

"Oh, my love, my love," Quinn knelt beside her and held her close. "What is the matter?"

She cried into his chest. "This is not who I wanted to be. I'm not cut out to be the executor of justice."

He was frightened about tomorrow, and about the days to follow. But in this moment, the rock of all the magical peoples in Elandria needed him to be strong. "You are, Amarice. No one could be a stronger leader than you."

"I'm frightened, Quinn."

"Me, too." He held her closer still. She turned her head up toward his and met his lips. He kissed her passionately.

"Make love to me," she whispered. And he did. He made love to her as if it were their last night on earth.

THE NEXT MORNING, Quinn and Amarice lay awake in their tent for a long time, intertwined and silent. They listened to the sounds of the guards cooking breakfast on the fire and packing up camp. Quinn held Amarice tightly, not wanting to let her go.

The day had dawned overcast and muggy. The thick air filled Quinn's lungs, making it hard to breathe. Between the humidity and the fear, Quinn wanted nothing more than to ride back to the safety of the Villa with Amarice. Their plan was sound, their guards well-trained, but Chambers did not sound like a man who would go quietly to his fate.

Quinn propped himself on his elbow and gazed at the woman next to him. He remembered the devastation she had rained down upon her kidnappers and felt some of his unease subside. The Sage herself had taught Quinn powerful earth magic, and he felt certain that if her life were threatened, Quinn could use his magic to protect her. Although, he thought, she likely would not need his protection, which made him love her even more.

Amarice spoke for the first time that morning. "I suppose we should get up." Her joints creaked as she pulled herself upright, and she groaned. "If all goes well, then the guards can take Charles back to Teleah, and we can sleep in an inn tonight."

Quinn smiled at the prospect of a warm bath to soothe his aching muscles and a plush bed for sleeping. He pulled on his tunic and pants and tossed Amarice her riding clothes. She shook her head. "No, I have to be the Sage today." She reached for her satchel and removed a forest green, gauzy dress and her diadem. Quinn watched her with adoration as she dressed in the cramped tent, pinning the dress on her shoulders, combing her hair, positioning the diadem on top of her head. No matter her apprehension from last night, she was born for this role.

Though it was early in the day, the guards wiped sweat from their brows as they ate their breakfast of sausage and crusty bread. Quinn smiled proudly when the men's jaws dropped as Amarice exited the tent. Even in the sweltering heat and sleeping in a tent for a week, Amarice was stunning. Her neckline plunged, and the nearly sheer material flowed over her hips. Her eyes sparkled, complementing the deep green of her dress. Most of these guards had never seen the Sage in all her glory, and she stood like a light against the grey skies.

Marcus handed Quinn and her each a tin plate of sausage and bread, and Amarice took her place in the circle with the guards, chatting with a nonchalance Quinn could never hope to achieve. He sat next to her in silence. Raymond joined them shortly, dressed in the royal colors, his family's sigil embroidered on his chest. He, too, had shifted into his formal role, and today his face held no laughter.

The prince reviewed their plan over breakfast. They would move closer to the village of Headham and wait until Charles' daily church service was over in the evening. Then, they would approach and formally arrest him. The plan was flawless, although no one felt it would be that simple.

Headham was only a two-hour ride away, so the muggy morning

held no sense of urgency, only a lingering apprehension of what the evening would bring.

While the guards packed up camp, Amarice stood some distance away, gazing off into the horizon. Quinn approached her and stood a foot behind, watching the beads of sweat roll down her neck and over her back. "Have you replenished your Gift?" she asked him without turning to look at him.

"Yes."

She sighed. "Hopefully, we will not need to use any earth magic."

"Do you find that likely?"

"No." She turned finally and took his hand. "But it never hurts to have hope." She stood on her toes to kiss Quinn's lips softly. "Shall we go?"

✿❧✿

THE COMPANY RODE the remaining few miles off the main road. Their plan would be foiled if Chambers was tipped off and fled. Or worse, if he rallied the village to his cause, and they were met with pitchforks and axes. They encountered no other people on their journey, and for the most part, they were silent.

Quinn rode next to Amarice and wondered how so much evil had infiltrated Elandria with no warning. He thought back to the first night he had awoken with such a terrible sense of doom. Nearly a year ago, now, and so much had changed. Had this darkness always existed in Elandria? He knew far too well that magic was often treated with suspicion in small villages like his own. But he would never have imagined the villagers he knew would resort to murder. Or would they? Had he lived in a bubble of Scholars for too long?

Just outside Headham, they stopped to wait in the cover of trees. One of the guards changed into plainclothes to keep watch in town. He would bring word to the others when the church service ended and the crowds had dispersed.

The forest darkened as the sun set, beams of red and orange light shining through the treetops. Quinn sat on the forest floor with Amarice in his lap. Raymond paced, muttering obscenities. Marcus tried to ease the mood by sharing stories from his career as Chief Inquisitor. It did little to help, despite the man's best intentions.

An hour after the sky had turned dark, the guard had returned. "It's time," he said. They followed him on foot into the town. Quinn held Amarice's hand the entire way, whether to give her strength or receive it, he did not know.

They stood a hundred yards outside the church and waited for the last of the villagers to leave. By Marcus' intelligence, Charles Chambers would still be in the church chatting with his closest members. Thunder rumbled overhead, a summer storm imminent. Fitting, Quinn thought.

As they drew closer to the church, Amarice let go of Quinn's hand. She lifted her hand to the wind when the group approached the door and blew it open with magic. Quinn raised an eyebrow at her under the streetlamp. She shrugged. "I've got a flair for the dramatic."

They entered the church behind Amarice. Six men dressed in long, black robes had turned in shock at the blown-open door. Quinn knew instantly which man was Charles. He was tall, with brown hair and dark eyes. He wore an ostentatious pendant of gold, no doubt paid for by his loyal subjects. His presence was commanding, but he paled in comparison to Amarice.

The Sage spoke. "Charles Chambers. I am Amarice Teyvana, Sage of Elandria. We have come to arrest you to stand trial for your crimes." She walked further down the aisle of the church, and her company followed.

Charles' men drew weapons, swords and axes. But their leader sighed and gestured for his cronies to lower them. They looked as shocked as Amarice's group. "I knew this was coming," the man said in a deep bass. "Carry on, then."

Amarice turned and motioned toward the Chief Inquisitor. Marcus cut a length of rope from his pouch and approached the man. He stood behind Charles and told him to put his hands behind his back so he could be tied. For a moment, it looked as though he would go willingly.

But he grabbed something from his pulpit as he lowered his hands. It happened too quickly for Marcus to react. Charles plunged a dagger into Marcus' abdomen. Amarice screamed, as Charles turned and stabbed Marcus once more through the heart. "I knew this was coming," he said again, evil in his voice.

Raymond drew his sword and rushed forward, followed by the guardsmen. He was met by the armed cronies, who were skilled enough to keep the guardsmen at bay. Charles stood watching, searching for a way to escape. But there was only one exit.

One of the guards fell to his death, hacked by a villager's axe. Blood stained the wooden benches. Quinn's heart pounded, and he grabbed Amarice by the wrist. He was desperate to protect her.

But Amarice pulled away, no longer shocked by the death. Her eyes turned dark, and green magic emanated from her entire body. The earth shook violently at her command. Everyone lost their balance as the walls shook and began to crumble.

"KILL HER!" Charles yelled as a large beam fell at his feet. One of his men feigned Raymond's sword and darted down the aisle toward Amarice.

Quinn did not even think. Red bolts of magic shot out of his hand toward the nearest lamp. The glass vase burst and Quinn pulled the fire through the air and set Amarice's attacker on fire. The man screamed in agony as the flames consumed him.

The distraction was enough to slow the others, and Raymond had the opportunity to plunge his sword through one of the men. Two more dropped their weapons in surrender. Only one remained, and he edged his way closer to Charles, who crouched, shaking, dagger in hand.

"Give up, Charles." Amarice's voice was a mix of a command and a beg. "No one else needs to die tonight."

"You do," Charles replied. He returned to a standing position, confidence returning. "All of you deserve to answer for your sins to the gods."

"Our sins?" Amarice laughed. "Like the sins of slaughtering unarmed Scholars and Deyoni?"

"They are demon workers. The earth must be cleansed of the demons."

Recognizing a lost cause, Amarice shifted her focus on the last man guarding Charles. His eyes were wide with fear. He was no fighter, and Amarice knew it. "Your friends have fallen, and you are left protecting a man who will not fight his own battles. He is a coward. He does not deserve your bravery." Her voice softened. "Lower your weapon, and you can go home to your family."

The man kept axe in hand, but they could see the internal conflict on his face. At that moment, rain fell through the destroyed ceiling of the church. The lamps went out; only the ball of Quinn's fire stayed lit by his magic, floating in the air. Finally, as if the rain answered his questions, the man began to lower his axe. "Traitor!" Charles plunged his dagger upward through the back of his skull. The man crumbled.

Amarice's anger manifested into wild magic. The rain became a torrential downpour, and the earth shook once more. More beams fell from the ceiling, and the walls began to crack. Quinn's fire grew in response to Amarice's own magic, and he struggled to control it. A single flame leapt from the air in front of him and set a wooden bench on fire. The blaze grew quickly, and they now stood in a burning building that even the storm could not quell.

"Amarice," Quinn said. Soon the situation would be too dangerous for even the source of the magic. She turned at the sound of his voice, dragging her out of her angry thoughts. The storm calmed some, and the fire slowed. Quinn and Raymond used their own Gift to calm the fire that the Sage no longer controlled.

She stepped back and urged the others in her party to do the same. "Stay behind me," she said as she edged backward toward the door. Amarice raised a hand to the sky. Electricity crackled from her hands and called to the lightning above. With a sharp drop, a bolt of lightning struck at Charles' feet, missing him by inches. The ground burst into flame.

Charles laughed. "Fool! The gods protect me." He leapt over the line of flame and charged Amarice. Quinn jumped in front of her and tackled the man. Amarice screamed.

Quinn punched him and pinned his wrist to the ground. He held his other hand at Charles' throat, cutting off air until he released the dagger. Quinn took the dagger and held it over the man.

Charles laughed. "It doesn't matter. This will not end with me. The gods will have their justice."

"And I will have mine." Filled with anger over Rafe's murder, Amarice's kidnapping, and the death of those in their party, Quinn slit the man's throat. He stood, dropping the dagger with a clamor.

Amarice threw her arms around her lover. "You idiot! Why didn't you just use magic? Why didn't you just let me use magic?" But she held him in a tight embrace as the church crumbled and burned around them.

He held her close. "They killed Rafe without magic. They attacked you without magic."

Amarice nodded and lay her head against his chest. "Don't do anything like that ever again."

Raymond spoke for the first time. "We're going to burn alive if we do not leave now!" The company followed the prince from the building. They stopped a few yards outside, watching the flames. Amarice waved an arm and slowed the storm to a slight drizzle. By this time, the villagers had gathered in fear. Screams of grief punctured the night.

Quinn stood with his arm around Amarice. "Should we stop the fire?"

"No. Let the dead return to the earth." Her eyes searched the grounds for something. A few yards away, the church's cemetery was lined by large chrysanthemum plants. She walked toward them and urged them to bloom, as it was not quite the right season. The buds burst into vibrant colors of red and yellow. She gathered two in her hands and walked toward the church. She spoke the names of the Chief Inquisitor and the fallen guard and tossed the flowers into the fire. The rest of the party followed suit.

Slowly, the villagers gathered flowers and tossed them into the flames, as well. After a long time, Amarice broke the grief-filled silence. "Let's go home."

CHAPTER 25

 *few months later...*

QUINN RETURNED to the Villa from his morning run and stopped in the southern garden, gazing at the Consort's Tree. The leaves had turned to gold, a glimmer against the horizon of reds and oranges. He had never seen the earth so beautiful as autumn in the Sage's Mountains.

He had left Amarice sleeping in the bed, as usual, for she loathed his early hours. At least she had learned to stay asleep as he dressed himself for his run. On his way out of the Villa this morning, Madge had stopped him to ask for a decision between beef and lamb for the first Harvest Holiday dinner that night. Guests would be arriving soon for the festivities, and she needed to begin cooking, she had explained to him. Quinn decided on beef.

Now, standing in the gardens, his mind clear from his run, he mused on the trivial exchange. Somehow, he had become an authority in the house, second only to Amarice. It had been a silent transition. Quinn had never been a leader before.

Nearly a year had passed since he first came to the Villa. Too many had died at the hands of Chambers and his followers. Quinn had learned to harness his immense power and had helped the Sage, the love of his life, defeat him. The last few months had passed without event. He had fallen into a happy pattern with Amarice. And now, he made decisions about food and place-settings and the grounds at the Sage's Villa. The day he received his letter about his apprenticeship seemed eons ago.

"What's on your mind, my love?" A sweet, sleepy voice lifted him from his thoughts. He turned to see Amarice walking toward him, barefoot in a thin dress of mauve. He smiled, as he did every time he saw her. Amarice joined him near the tree and slipped her arm around his waist. A chill had settled into the air, and she shivered.

He hugged her tightly. "Wondering who I have become in the last year. I barely recognize myself." He kissed the top of her head.

"And who do you think you have become?"

Quinn thought for a few moments. In this moment, everything felt right, as it had for the last few months. He had never felt more confident, more connected, and more loved than he did now. He answered her, a strength in his voice never heard a year ago.

"Myself."

Amarice grinned. She knew all along who Quinn had the potential to become. He just had to find it himself. Quinn continued, "I found much of myself in you, Amarice. I cannot help but feel that our souls are so..." He searched for the right word. "... intertwined."

She nodded. "Like the Consort's Tree," she said, gesturing toward the two ancient trunks that wound around one another. "Quinn, I would like to give you your Harvest Day gift now."

An odd segue, he thought. Though the week-long Harvest Holiday began today, gifts were typically given on the fourth day at the grandest feast. "All right."

She stepped away from his embrace and faced him. "Do not feel obligated to accept, my love. It would change nothing between us." She met his confused eyes. "I have spoken with the king, and he agrees. After your commencement in a few weeks' time, you will fully be a Scholar in your own right." Her voice changed to a note of nervousness, an unusual tone for the Sage. "If you would accept, I would like to name you Sage's Consort."

Quinn waited for the punchline. It did not come. The Sage's Consort was a rare position, and despite their bliss as a couple, he had not expected this. The position would make him one of the most powerful diplomats in Elandria, in the world. He nearly laughed at the prospect; a few months ago he was a shy, insecure boy. "Are you certain?"

"I trust you with my whole heart. I adore you. And the country will benefit from your voice," she told him. "Do you accept?"

He let himself laugh now. "Yes! A hundred times yes!" He swept her into his arms and kissed her with a burning passion. "I love you."

"I love you, my Lord Consort."

He laughed again. He had a title. He carried her back to their chambers, and they did not leave their shared bed for several hours.

❧

THE HARVEST HOLIDAY was the happiest week Quinn had ever known. The Villa was packed with guests, and every day was filled with feasts and games and dancing. Although his title would not be official until after his commencement in two weeks' time, Amarice introduced him to everyone as Sage's Consort.

Jack stayed at the Villa for the holiday. He had two investors willing to pay his rent on a shop for a year, and he had found a place on the main road, near the market, to start his apothecary business. It would open just after the Feast of Fire, on the first day of the new year. He was more reserved than he had been in school, but Quinn knew he still grieved over Rafe and his unspoken love.

Prince Raymond broke from tradition and celebrated the holiday at the Villa instead of the palace. He and Daisy had corresponded and met several times over the last few months. He was quite smitten. Raymond had become one of Quinn's closest friends, and Quinn's urges of jealousy became more and more fleeting.

Three tribes of Deyoni had made camp on the grounds to share in the Sage's celebrations. Most of the tribes from the Valley had begun to travel the countryside again, after the defeat of Chambers, but a few lingered. These three tribes were the only to accept Amarice's invitation, and they put on shows for all the guests several times a day. Quinn spent several hours of the holiday in their camps, practicing his budding knowledge of the Deyoni language, and, though he tried to deny it to himself, looking for his father. "We will find him. One day," Amarice assured him.

On the fourth day, Harvest Day, they feasted from sunup to sundown. Amarice and the Deyoni women who worked at the Villa performed traditional dances, working the dance magic on the entire crowd.

Later, a hired orchestra played, and Quinn danced for hours with Amarice, pausing only to drink or eat more. After several drinks, he and his love sat on a bench, eating chocolate pastries and watching the crowd as the autumn sun set.

A young woman in blue Messenger garb pushed through the crowd. She handed Amarice a letter. "For you, my lady," she said before disappearing without another word. Amarice looked at Quinn, confused. Messengers only worked on Harvest Holiday in case of emergency, but the woman had disappeared.

She opened the letter, closed with only a generic seal. Her eyes widened, and she handed the letter to Quinn. Only four words were written: "SINNER, IT'S NOT OVER."

They searched for the Messenger, but she was gone. Amarice and Quinn left the party and disappeared into her study. "What does it mean? Has there been another attack?"

"I don't know," Amarice said. "But right now, I don't care." He looked at her, surprised. "It's Harvest Day. I'm not scared, and I have you. I'll worry later."

He took her in his arms and kissed her. "You're right." He glanced at the door that led to their room. "I don't think anyone will miss us if we stay gone a little longer."

Amarice grinned, and he took her to bed. An hour later, Amarice lay asleep in his arms as he stroked her hair. He breathed in her scent of rose and kissed her brow. In two weeks, he would not only be a fully qualified Scholar, but he would also gain the title of Sage's Consort.

And the woman who held his future lay in his arms. The insecure, stifled boy he had been when he received his letter in Quickthorn's office was gone.

Quinn smiled and sighed, breathing in the contentment that can come only with a sense of belonging.